Praise
Christmas is the Girl Next Door

"A gloriously sweet holiday read about expectations and reality."
—*Kirkus Reviews*

"A town called Christmas. An iffy wish come true. A new girl who could change it all. *All I Want For Christmas Is The Girl Next Door* kept me on my toes, turning pages from the start, and loving each revelation as it unfolded. Deep, funny, and real—this holiday romance will completely warm your heart and remind you that not all wishes should come true."
—Nova McBee, author of the *Calculated* Series

"Full of charm, wit, and so much warmth, Bobulski's *All I Want For Christmas Is The Girl Next Door* will have you breaking out in Christmas carols and will melt even the coldest heart!"
—Erin A. Craig, NYT Bestselling Author of
House of Salt and Sorrows

"A cozy winter read you'll want to wrap yourself in like a blanket. At once bittersweet and hopeful, Bobulski thoughtfully explores the question of whether what we want is truly what we need against a backdrop of snowflakes, Christmas floats, and plenty of fresh cookies. A timeless holiday classic."
—Natalie Mae, author of *The Kinder Poison*

"This story is as magical as a shooting star on a cold winter night. Chelsea Bobulski's thoughtful and romantic exploration of true love and destiny will have readers swooning and wishing for her next Christmas novel!"
—Kristy Boyce, author of *Hot British Boyfriend*

"A fun frolic through the most wonderful time of the year! Full of heart and humor, this lighthearted twist on being careful what you wish for sparkles with delightful dialogue, swoony romance, and an ending that tugs at your heart before making it soar. Bobulski makes you think about being so focused on what we want that we miss what we already have. A holiday must-read!"

—Lori Goldstein, author of *Love, Theodosia, Sources Say,* and *Screen Queens*

"The charm of a small-town Hallmark Christmas meets the longing and wish fulfillment of John Green's Paper Towns in this magical holiday read. Expertly woven with strings of romance, ribbons of hope, and the sparkling power of gratitude, *All I Want For Christmas Is The Girl Next Door* is the perfect holiday story to curl up with on a snowy day. I adored every page!"

— Lorie Langdon, best-selling author of *Doon,* and *Olivia Twist*

"This is the book equivalent of drinking a mug of hot chocolate while listening to Christmas music as snowflakes gently fall outside. An all-around comforting, hopeful, and festive holiday read that will make you feel as cozy as your favorite Christmas movies."

—Kerry Winfrey, author of *Waiting for Tom Hanks*

All I Want For Christmas is
the girl next door

CHELSEA BOBULSKI

 WISE WOLF BOOKS LAS VEGAS

WISE WOLF
BOOKS

This is a work of fiction. All of the characters, organizations, publications, and events portrayed in this novel are either products of the author's imagination or are used fictitiously.

For information, address Wolfpack Publishing,
5130 S. Fort Apache Road, 215-380 Las Vegas, NV 89148
wisewolfbooks.com

Cover design by Wise Wolf Books

ISBN 978-1-953944-11-5 (paperback) 978-1-953944-10-8 (ebook)
LCCN: 2021937075

First Edition: October 2021

All I Want

For Christmas is

the girl next door

To Emerson and Caleb—May you always know the path that leads you Home.

1

* * *

I live in a small town. The kind of small where if you bet me yours was smaller, I'd probably win.

You only know it's small if you're a townie. The tourists always make it seem bigger than it actually is, especially this time of year. But I know exactly how small it is because six days a week, I deliver newspapers to ninety-four houses scattered across six streets. Another kid from my high school takes the other eighty. Granted, not everyone gets the morning paper, so the population can't be totaled on those houses alone, but you get the picture.

Not the smallest town in America, but small enough.

I started delivering newspapers in seventh grade. Back then, I rode my bike unless it was snowing, raining, or below freezing. On those days, my dad would get up at four o'clock every morning just to drive me across town. We always stopped for doughnuts on the way home, making sure to get at least one chocolate-glazed for the last house on my route.

Sarah Clarke's house.

It's still a tradition. Every Friday morning, Sarah and I cel-ebrate the end of the week with a box of chocolate-glazed, and this Friday is no exception. I pull Dad's car into my driveway, a white box cradled in the seat next to me.

Sarah's already waiting for me on her front stoop. She's wearing black leggings and a puffy coat. Her hair's pulled back into the ponytail she wears for yoga, which she'll twist up into a bun later for ballet. She holds a pink ther-mos with a rhinestone crown, the words *Dancing Queen* scribbled across it. Next to her is a blue thermos she picked up for me at a store in Williamsburg that says, *Bookworms Do It Better*.

When she first showed it to me, I told her it was obscene. She said it was only obscene if I chose to read it that way.

"The 'it' in that statement could be anything," she ar-gued. "Laundry. You could do laundry better. Or skiing. Or cross-country running. It can be anything you want it to be."

"What I *want* it to be," I replied, "is obscene."

She laughed in that way that always makes my heart feel like someone's smashing it with a hammer. "Typical high school boy."

So, anyway, that's our deal. I bring the doughnuts. She brings the coffee.

I park the car, grab the twine-wrapped bakery box from the passenger seat, walk across our yard, and hop the white picket fence, my boots cracking the frosted grass beneath me.

"You know, there is a gate you can use," Sarah tells me, handing me my thermos as I hand her the box. "You don't have to Indiana Jones it over the fence every time."

I blinked. "But then how will you know I'm studly and likely to outrun a boulder?"

She shakes her head. "How you don't have a girlfriend

is beyond me."

Ouch.

What I want to say—what I absolutely *cannot* say—is that the only reason I don't have a girlfriend is because the girl I love is dating my best friend, Jeremy Davis. Which means she's completely off-limits, even though a part of me has been in love with her since she moved into the house next door almost ten years ago.

For the record, I'm trying to get over her.

We devour our sugar-glazed, fried morsels of heaven in silence—there's no room for talking when hot dough-nuts are getting colder by the second. A dog barks down the street. A cold breeze skitters across the leaves in Sarah's yard, making her shiver. I scoot closer, so our arms and legs are touching. She leans into my warmth with a small sigh and pops the last bite into her mouth, then takes a napkin from the box and wipes the glaze from her fingers.

"Thanks for this," she says. "I've been up half the night studying for MacGregor's test."

"Ah, the Civil War." I shudder. "So many battlefields. So many dates."

She bumps me with her shoulder. "Okay, Mr. Perfect GPA. I'm pretty sure you've had every battle memorized since you were eight."

"Well, you know, Indiana Jones isn't just studly. He's an academic."

She laughs. "You just let me know if you ever need some-one to rescue you from the Nazis."

"You'll be the first one I call."

"I better be." She reaches for my thermos. I take one last sip before handing it over.

"See you in a few," I say as she turns to go inside, the silver bells on her front wreath tinkling as she opens and closes her door.

I take a deep breath, watching the door for a second longer than I should, then jump back over the fence and head up my own front walkway.

I check the time on my phone—5:30—and set an alarm for 6:30 as I climb the stairs to my room. Keeping the lights off, I throw my phone on my bedside table, kick off my shoes, and tell myself not to do the next thing, but I can't help it:

I glance out my window, checking to see if Sarah's bedroom light is on.

When we were kids, that light was a source of comfort, as if the simple fact that Sarah Clarke was still there—still in her pink bedroom with the white-doily curtains and the slanted ceiling—meant that, no matter what was happening, everything would be okay. It still comforts me, but there's also an ache attached to it now, because I know she looks for my light too, and yet whatever connection we have that makes us seek each other out like moths to a flame, it isn't enough to make her choose me.

Her light blinks on. Knowing her, she's going over her notes for MacGregor's test again.

I tell myself not to think about her as I lie down in bed and close my eyes, but it's like telling myself not to breathe. Her face is imprinted on my eyelids. She is the first thing I see every morning and the last thing I see every night.

✳✳✳

I wake to the voice of Gene Autry singing "Here Comes Santa Claus" a full nineteen minutes before my alarm is set to go off. I groan and try to block out the music with my pillow, but that smooth-toned, Christmas-loving cowboy croons straight through the floorboards. Growling, I unfold my pillow, press my thumb and forefinger into my eyes, and switch off the alarm on my phone.

I get up slowly, my spine cracking as I swing my legs over the side of my bed. It's the price I always pay this time of year, when my hours at the bookstore double to meet the demand of the holiday crowd that flocks to our small but famous town of Christmas, Virginia. Not that I'm complaining. More hours mean more money, and Aunt Bee (not my real aunt, just a nice old lady who never had any kids herself) is always generous with the holiday bonus. Still, getting up at four o'clock every morning to deliver the paper, followed by five hours of standing and bending and heavy lifting at the bookstore every night after school, is definitely taking its toll. I'm basically a ninety-year-old man trapped inside a sixteen-year-old body.

Sexy, I know.

Mom worries I'm taking on too much, and she's probably right, but she and Dad can't pay for college and the only way I'm making it out of this town is by saving up as much money as I can now so I don't get swallowed up by student loans I'll never be able to repay.

After showering, I change into jeans and a thermal shirt, stuff my books into my backpack, and head downstairs. That God-given aroma of freshly brewed coffee mixes with the smell of sugar cookies baking in the oven and the scent of the cinnamon holiday wall plugs strewn throughout the house. It's what I imagine the North Pole would smell like, minus the elf sweat and reindeer musk.

The kitchen's decked out in vintage Coca-Cola Christmas posters, along with twin mini-trees with twinkle lights on either side of the patio door, a bouquet of poinsettias in the middle of the breakfast table, and boughs of holly hanging from the light fixture. The radio switches to Bing Crosby singing "I'll Be Home for Christmas" as I cross to the coffeemaker and pour myself one of the to-go cups Mom keeps stashed in the cupboard for guests.

Mom side-eyes me from the kitchen island as she sifts dry ingredients into a bowl. Her apron and half the counter is covered in flour. "Graham."

I arch a brow. "Mother."

"Didn't we have this conversation yesterday?"

I pop the lid onto the thermos, cutting off those delicious swirls of caffeinated steam. "You mean the one where you said I was too young to drink coffee, and I said I'd stop drinking it as soon as you started paying me in allowance what I make at the bookstore, that way I could take naps in the afternoons and be completely useless to society?"

Mom nods. "That's the one."

"Has anything changed on that front?"

"Nope," she says, clapping flour off of her hands and turning back to her mixer. "How about you?"

I snag a cookie from the cooling rack. "Not a chance."

Mom swats at my hand. "Those are for the church bake sale."

"I'll put an extra dollar in the offering this week." I bite into the cookie, which is pure heaven masquerading as saturated fat. I grab one more from the rack. "Make that two dollars."

She shakes her head. "What am I going to do with you?"

"Well, if you figure it out, you'll have to tell me later. I'm late for school. Oh, wait, no I'm not. I'm early, thanks to a private serenade by the one and only Gene Autry."

"You know, I would tell you I'm sorry about that, but I just have a hard time lying to my own son."

"You wound me, woman."

"Take an umbrella with you. It's supposed to rain tonight."

"Yeah, yeah," I say, heading for the entryway. "See you later."

"No goodbye hug?"

"Why don't you ask your boyfriend Gene?"

"She would if she could, son," Dad says as he starts down the staircase, the seventy-year-old steps creaking along with his knees. "She would if she could."

I open the front door, waving vaguely over my shoulder. "Later, Pops."

"Have a good day at school," he calls back. "Don't do anything I wouldn't do."

I shake my head as I step out onto the porch and close the door behind me, sleigh bells jingling on the handle. I take another bite of the sugar cookie, making it look less like a star and more like a three-legged octopus. The sugar cubes dissolve on my tongue, and even though I sometimes wonder what it would have been like to have grown up in a normal town—one that isn't obsessed with Christmas 365 days a year—I can't pretend to be like some of the other jaded kids I go to school with, the ones who think it's cooler to hate Christmas than to buy into all the hype. Not when I'm chomping down on homemade sugar cookies, or when the holiday rush puts sweet, sweet overtime in my pocket, or even when Mom blasts Christmas music at indecent hours.

Christmas is my favorite time of the year because it's Sarah Clarke's favorite time of the year too.

I bound down the front steps, and there she is, leaning against her white picket fence, the early morning light painting the trees and grass around her silver blue. Her dark hair is pulled into a bun, just like I knew it would be, and she's wearing fuzzy pink earmuffs that match her gloves. Her nose and cheeks are the color of bubblegum, and when she looks up at me, all I can think is:

Perfect.

She's perfect.

Perfect can get boring, you know.

I don't know why the voice of Piper Hudson, the new girl in town, randomly pops into my head. She hadn't even been talking to me when she said it—she'd been in a group of her fellow cheerleaders at the front of the bookstore, sliding her finger along the spines in the new arrivals section as her friends gossiped about some college guys they'd met in Williamsburg. I didn't even think she was listening to them, she was so focused on the books, methodically pulling one out and exchanging it for another.

She's definitely one of my more fascinating customers to watch. She never buys more than one book per visit, and she agonizes over the decision even though she and I both know she'll be back the same time next week to buy the book she left behind.

Maybe it was something in the way she'd said it—*Perfect can get boring, you know*—the absolute certainty and hint of regret in her voice, like she was genuinely sorry to be the one to tell them, that made me look up from my homework. Still, it's weird that those words would come back to me now, when the epitome of perfection is standing right in front of me, especially when Sarah Clarke is anything but boring.

Shoving all random thoughts of Piper Hudson out of my mind, I amble down the stone pavers of our front walkway, dark and slick from the overnight rain, through the front gate, and onto the sidewalk.

"Cookie?" I offer, holding up the second one.

Sarah groans. "Why, why, *why* would you bring that out here?"

"Because it's delicious."

"Exactly. You know I can't say no to baked goods, especially your mom's." She rolls her eyes and shoves the cookie into her mouth. "Ugh, that should be illegal." She claps the crumbs off her mittens. "And now between the doughnut and the cookie, I'm going to have a sugar high through English and then crash just in time to forget everything about the Civil War."

"Don't act like you didn't have one of those disgusting kale smoothies for breakfast."

"What does that have to do with anything?"

We start down the sidewalk, and in this, in the cadence of our steps, in the slight brushing of our arms as we walk, in the jostling of our backpacks, there's a rhythm that's been ours and ours alone for the past decade. It's familiar and comforting and heartbreaking all at once, because I know it's fleeting. In two more years, she'll still be with Jeremy, and I'll be gone.

"Kale cancels out sugar," I tell her.

"You're making that up."

"Pretty sure I'm not."

"Well, if that's true, I'm going to start putting one of those 'disgusting kale smoothies', in your thermos every morning instead of coffee."

My eyes narrow. "You wouldn't dare."

"Stop making fun of my kale."

"You drive a hard bargain, Miss Clarke."

"It's one of my many talents." She grins and hitches her thumbs around her backpack straps. "So, did you get a date to the winter formal yet?"

"I've still got a couple weeks, if I even want to go."

"What do you mean?"

"I was thinking I might skip it this year."

"You can't! You skipped it last year."

"I don't think having bronchitis constitutes 'skipping it'. I would have gone if it weren't for all the death rattling."

"Whatever. You're going this year."

"Says who?"

"Says me."

"You, uh . . ." *Don't ask, don't ask, don't ask—* "You really want me there?"

"Duh." She elbows me in the side. "Besides, Jeremy wants

to rent one of Mr. Hanover's carriages and it's cheaper if another couple splits the cost."

"So, you're after me for my money."

"Hey, I could have asked anyone, but I'm asking you. That counts for something, right?"

I force a smile. "Sure."

We turn onto Main Street, heading away from the town square and the small independent shops that make our town "the place to visit for family holiday fun". The old-fashioned lampposts dotting either side of the street wink out as a bus hisses by, tingeing the air with exhaust.

"So?" Sarah asks. "How about it?"

"How about what?"

"The dance."

"Oh, uh—"

Three fully-formed options slam into my brain all at once, and I'm not sure which one to go with. I can tell her the truth, which is that I don't really want to go to some dance where I'll have to watch her make out with my best friend all night and have to listen to how much they love each other and have to hear from other people how *perfect* they are together. I get enough of that in my everyday life as it is.

I can tell her I already promised Mom I'd help her make apple pies for the nursing home or whatever other Christmas-y thing she'll be doing that night while Dad shouts all the wrong answers to *Jeopardy* in the background.

Or, option three, I can man up and find someone to take.

"If you need a date," she says, her eyes wide, which is how I know what she's about to say can't be good, "my cousin Dina's going to be visiting with her family. I know she'd love to go."

"*Dina?* Isn't she in seventh grade?"

"Eighth, actually, but she's the oldest in her class—"

"Save it," I say, trying to ignore the gaping pit where my

stomach used to be. Is this really what she thinks of me? That my charm and overall attractiveness are in such short supply that I need her to set me up on a date with her *thirteen-year-old cousin*? The only thing worse would be taking my own sister. Thank God I don't have one.

Out of annoyance, I open my mouth and say probably the dumbest thing I've ever said in my whole pathetic, dateless life: "I've already got someone in mind."

Yep, that's what I said. Not *the dance is lame* or *my family's going out of town* or *I need to wash my hair* or any of the other excuses people have been coming up with for decades to avoid dressing up and parading around for the entire school to heckle. Nope, what I decided to say was: *I've already got someone in mind.*

"You do?" Sarah asks. "Who?"

I scoff loud enough for the sound to bounce off the decorative trumpet of a six-foot angel in the yard next to us and reverberate back into my ear. "You don't want to ruin the surprise, do you?"

"Okay, well, you better get a move on before someone else asks her."

Too late, I think as our school rises up in front of us. I glance around at the other kids filing through the front doors, my heart ratcheting up my throat at the thought of asking some random girl to the dance. But the last thing I need is a pity date, especially with the thirteen-year-old cousin of the girl I've been in love with for the past decade.

Besides, how hard can it be to find a date to a dance that's still two weeks away?

2

***

Very hard, apparently.

There are only forty-three kids in my class, so it took all of four periods to figure out that almost everyone paired up for the dance all the way back in October.

"You've got to ask early. How else do you expect a girl to know if she should go dress shopping or not?" Jamie Kipp told me after turning me down in third period study hall.

"Good point," I said, although I have no idea why dress shopping should take two months.

Which is how I've found myself behind the register at the bookstore, hunched over xeroxed copies of my sophomore yearbook as Jeremy sits on the edge of the counter, tossing gummy bears into the air and catching them on his tongue. There are black Xs through the pictures of each girl who has turned me down already, making an efficient—if slightly creepy—index of my many rejections. Next to them sits a piece of paper listing everything I know about the three girls I haven't asked yet.

1. Amanda Crumb: self-identified "band geek", loves camping, smells nice, probably out of my league
2. Kayla Yu: daughter of a millionaire, dating the quarterback of Virginia Tech, definitely out of my league
3. Piper Hudson: new girl, loves books, cheerleader, thinks perfect is boring, stupendously out of my league

Any luck?" Jeremy asks, popping a gummy bear into the air and swerving to the right. The bear bounces off his nose and lands on the faded blue carpet. He picks it up and frowns. It's covered in dust speckles and lint.

I take the gummy bear from him, throw it in the trash, and grab a candy cane from the miniature Christmas tree on the counter. "Put those things away and eat this instead. You're annoying me."

"Okay, Dad." Jeremy stuffs his half-eaten bag of gummy bears into the front pocket of his backpack and tears at the candy cane wrapper, breaking off a piece between his teeth with a loud *CRACK*. "*Hmmm*. Watermelon."

I roll my eyes and turn back to my yearbook.

"What are you going to all this trouble for? Sarah said you already had a date."

"No, I said I had someone in mind, but it . . . didn't work out."

"Oh." Jeremy grinds the candy against his molars. "Bummer."

That's an understatement.

I didn't really know it then, but, looking back, I've been in love with Sarah Clarke since the day she moved into the house next door. She stood in her new front yard, watching the moving men take cardboard boxes into the house with eyes that seemed too big for her head. She wore a pale-yellow dress with pink ballet slippers, and I remember thinking she looked like a lemon drop.

I wish I could say something amazing happened that made me finally realize I cared about her as more than a friend—a surprise kiss, maybe, or the sudden urge to sing about my feelings for her while swinging from a lamp-post and tap-dancing in the rain—but it was as simple as seeing her locker across from mine on the first day of freshman year.

She'd grown several inches over the summer, and her arms and legs were toned from her newfound yoga obsession, giving her the appearance of a fairy warrior princess who could just as easily slice your throat as perform *Swan Lake*. Her hair was longer too and streaked with gold from the sun. But it was her smile, as unchanging as the town itself, that did me in.

It must have done Jeremy in too because he's been dating her for the past two years. Of course, I was the idiot who let him. Not that Jeremy needed my permission or anything, but he had been nice enough to ask me if it was okay. At the time, I figured they'd last a week or two—maybe a month, if Jeremy could manage to keep his most annoying habits to himself. And then I would wait the appropriate amount of time to make sure Jeremy was over her before asking her out myself.

I'm still waiting.

"Let me see that," Jeremy says, grabbing the list. "Some good options here, but you might as well get rid of Kayla. She bought two tickets for the dance at lunch today."

"So?"

"So, she wouldn't buy *two* tickets if she didn't already have a date." He taps his finger against the notebook. "Probably bringing said quarterback boyfriend."

Well, there goes that option. It was a long shot anyway, but I had been hoping Kayla's boyfriend would consider himself above such lowly things as high school dances now that he's a major college football star.

I tug the notebook out from underneath Jeremy's sticky finger and strike a line through Kayla's name. "What about Amanda? She buy any tickets?"

"Not on my watch, but Sarah took over for me at the booth halfway through lunch so I could go argue with Mr. Carmichael, so I can't be sure."

"Still steamed about that D?"

"It's Art One, Graham. *Art One*. Who cares if my proportions were off by an eighth of an inch? I never claimed to be da Vinci or that guy—the one who cut off his ear?"

"Van Gogh?"

"Yeah, that creep. Besides, isn't art supposed to be subjective? Maybe I *wanted* the proportions to be off. Maybe I was making a statement about the injustice of soggy pizza dough in the cafeteria. Maybe I'm an abstract expressionist being forced into the harsh, cold box of realism."

"Did you tell Mr. Carmichael that?"

"Yeah, but he only bumped me up to a D-plus."

"I guess you're just doomed to be one of those artists people only appreciate posthumously."

"Guess so." Jeremy glances at his watch. "Speaking of, I've gotta run. I'm meeting Sarah at the diner later, and if I don't watch my sister for a couple hours first, my mom will kill me. Good luck with all of that." He gestures to the list before swinging his backpack onto his shoulder and loping through the front door. A gasp of cold air streams into the store, sprouting goosebumps on the back of my hands as I flip through the yearbook pictures one more time, contemplating our junior class and wondering just how many rejections a guy can take before he self-combusts.

Who am I kidding? I've asked out nearly every girl in my class, so even if by some miracle I could find someone in another class who (a) doesn't have a date yet and (b) doesn't mind going to the dance with a pathetic loser like me, everyone will know it was a last-ditch effort. Maybe in other high schools, where there are a thousand kids in each class, people don't care as much about that sort of thing, but I live in a town that could rival Whoville for the Smallest Bit of Square Footage People Have Ever Lived In. I will be known as that kid who couldn't get a date to the Winter Formal until I die.

The bell over the door tinkles as Piper Hudson pushes her way in, her blonde hair swept to the side by the wind, a few strands catching on her eyelashes. She runs her hand through her hair, trying to tame it, but her fingers get tangled in the knots.

"Shoot," she mumbles, using her free hand to hold her hair in place while she tries to extricate her knuckles. She glances up, and our eyes meet. Her cheeks redden. "Oh, hey."

"Hey."

"Windy out there."

"Yeah." I manage a smirk even though my stomach is suddenly doing flip tricks like it's trying out for the X Games. You'd think after asking out nearly every other girl in my class, I'd have gotten used to opening myself up to rejection hours ago. But now that the moment is here and Piper Hudson has become my last chance to get a date to the dance, my tongue dries up and the words pile up in my throat, refusing to budge.

Don't be an idiot. Just ask her. What's the worst she can say?

But before I can open my mouth, she strides forward, pulls her gloves off her hands, stuffs them in her jacket pockets, and asks, "Got anything new?"

"Since Monday? Let me check." I look pensively off into the distance. "Nope, sorry."

She chuckles. "Yeah, I figured."

"Like it matters," I say. "You're just going to pick up one of the books you ogled the last time you were here."

"Ah, so the jig is up."

"The jig was never really down to begin with."

Piper laughs.

I smile.

Then the moment ends and we're just staring at each other, but it isn't like when Sarah stares at me. It's uncomfortable and awkward, and we both keep opening our mouths, trying to come up with something to say. I tap my pen against the counter, leaving black marks on the antique wood. She clears her throat and brushes her hair out of her eyes. Then, as if in slow motion, her gaze follows my pen down to the copies of my yearbook and the list next to it. The list with her name.

Crap.

"What's that?" she asks.

Think of something clever. Think of something clever.

"My, uh ... little black book?"

"My name isn't crossed out."

"You haven't dated me yet." I wince even as the words tumble out of my mouth. *And the award for Douchebag Comment of the Year goes to—*

"You expect me to believe you've dated all these girls?"

"Ouch." I place my hand over my heart. "Are you *trying* to kill me?"

She shrugs and looks up at me from beneath her lashes. I've never been this close to her before. Never noticed her eyes are the exact same shade of gray as a winter sky.

"No." I clear my throat. "I haven't dated all of these girls. It's, uh ... it's kind of embarrassing."

Her eyebrows shoot up. "I could use an embarrassing story after the day I've had."

I drop my pen back into the Santa coffee mug perched

on the edge of the desk and close my notebook before she sees that too. "What happened?"

"Uh-uh. You first."

This is it. The moment of truth.

I take a deep breath. "I need a date for the winter formal. All the names crossed out already have dates or can't go. Or possibly just don't want to go with me."

Her brow furrows. "And I'm that far down the list?"

"No," I say, quickly. "I just figured a girl like you would already have a date."

She pushes away from the counter and crosses her arms over her chest, but she doesn't look angry. She looks . . . amused.

"What does that mean? A girl like me?"

"You know. Cheerleader. Popular. Hot. You can stop me anytime now."

"Anything else?"

"Uh . . . vertically challenged?"

She snorts. It's a very unattractive sound, the sort of sound Sarah would call unladylike, having been raised on the Debutante's Guide to Proper Behavior by her Alabama-born mother. But I find it endearing.

"Yeah," she says. "We short girls do tend to get around."

"Oh no, that's not what I—"

"Well, for your information, I don't have a date. I've only been here a month, and like you said, almost everyone else is paired up."

Is she saying what I think she's saying?

She leans against the Self-Help bookcase (ironic, seeing as I would love to know how to help myself from being such a loser right about now).

"So?" she asks.

"Hmm?"

"Are you going to ask me out, or what?"

"Would you, um . . ." I cross my arms over my chest, but it doesn't feel natural and I think I read somewhere that crossing your arms can give off the impression you're not interested, so I uncross them and hook my thumbs in my pockets instead. "Would you like to go to the dance with me?"

She curls her fingers into her palm and holds her hand up to the light, inspecting her nails. "Maybe."

"Maybe?"

"I need to think about it. I don't usually go out with guys who point out how short I am. It's kind of rude."

Her tone is sarcastic and her eyes are bright like she's joking, but I'm still not sure how to take her. She isn't nearly as straightforward as Sarah. Then again, I've known Sarah almost my entire life. I know when she's joking and when she's not, when her "fine" really means "fine" and when it means "I'm going to punch someone's lights out".

But Piper Hudson is a total mystery.

"Oh," I say. "Sorry?"

"Apology accepted. I'll get an answer back to you soon. Unless you'd rather take Amanda Crumb?"

"No. I mean, she's perfectly nice and all, and I'd be honored to take her, but I"—*Stop babbling*—"I'd rather take you."

The right side of her mouth curves up. "Okay, cool. I'll let you know."

"Okay. Cool."

"Okay." She fidgets back and forth on the balls of her feet. "I guess I'll go find that book now."

I nod.

She starts to turn away.

"Wait."

She glances back.

"You said you were having a bad day too?"

"It's nothing. Family drama." She shrugs and gives me a little smile, like it's no big deal. I can tell it's worse than she's letting on, but she's already disappearing into the stacks, and I don't push it.

A cloud of perfume lingers by the desk in her wake. It smells soft and timeless, like the jasmine that springs up in Mom's garden every year. Nothing at all like the typical vanilla or gingerbread perfume most girls wear this time of year.

My phone buzzes in my pocket. A text from Sarah:

SOS HELP!!! Can you come to Riddle's Bridal and help me pick out a dress for the winter formal? Can't decide between two, and I need to know which one Jeremy will like better. Pleeeeease???

My first thought, as it always is with Sarah, is a resounding YES. Usually just the chance to see her, to be alone with her, to hear her voice and see her smile, is enough for me to forgo any other commitment and run to her side. But even as I'm doing it, even when I'm filled with so much excitement I can barely contain myself, my heart is also shattering, because I'm willing to give up anything and everything to be with her, but she isn't willing to do the same for me.

She's choosing a dress for Jeremy. Not me.

Yeah, that testosterone-laden, lovesick voice in the back of my head whispers, but she could have asked anyone for help. She has a bunch of friends she could have gone dress shopping with. She's asking you. Doesn't that count for something?

I drop my phone onto the counter and run my hands over my face. This right here is exactly why I work so hard at the bookstore, why I've kept the paper route instead of handing it off to some unsuspecting, idealistic seventh grader. I need to save up enough money so I can go to college somewhere far, far away. New York, maybe, or Chicago. Somewhere with a crowd I can get lost in, where I can reinvent myself and meet new people who know absolutely nothing about me. Somewhere no one's ever heard of Sarah Clarke, where memories of her aren't imprinted on every street corner and in every store.

A place where I can finally move on.

Sarah and Jeremy are townies. They both want to go to William & Mary, the closest college at only thirty minutes away, and then they want to get married and have babies and stay in Christmas, Virginia the rest of their lives, and there's no reason to think it won't happen that way.

My only hope for survival is to leave.

But the financial aspect isn't really the problem. I've been saving up for years, and come graduation, I should have enough for a used car and one year of tuition and boarding (maybe a little more if I go where the cost of living is cheap). I'll keep a job through college, and I just might be able to get a four-year degree without much in the way of student loans.

No, the hardest part will be severing all ties with Sarah (and Jeremy, by extension). At least until I can honestly say I'm over her.

But today isn't that day.

I glance at the clock, then text back:

No problem. Store closes in twenty. Be there soon.

3

***

I lock up fast after Piper leaves, counting the money in the register, turning off the lights, locking the front door, and pulling the gate over the door and windows shut within the span of six minutes.

Mom was right. It's raining, a light mist I can barely feel on my skin, creating halos around the lampposts lining the path and the white Christmas lights swirling up them. The trees on the square aren't decorated yet—the town saves that for the annual Christmas toy drive and tree-decorating contest—but the speakers rigged up in the trees and outside all of the shops are playing the same radio station Mom was listening to this morning.

Riddle's Bridal Boutique is located in the old firehouse on the north corner of the town square, and my heart skips a beat the second my gaze lands on it.

I hate that I want to see her this badly. Hate the hope that always pops up, that maybe *this* will be the time she finally realizes *I'm* the one she's supposed to be with. The guy she's been waiting for all along.

I stop outside the boutique and wipe my shoes on the welcome mat. Sarah spots me through the window and waves me in.

"So?" she asks as I walk through the door. "What do you think?"

She's wearing a long silver dress that slinks down her willowy dancer's frame like mercury. Her hair's down and wavy after taking it out of the bun she wore for practice, she doesn't have a drop of makeup on, and she is the most beautiful thing I have ever seen.

"You, uh—" I clear my throat. "I mean, you look . . ."

Her eyes widen. "Wow. That must be pretty good, huh?"

I nod, not trusting myself to speak.

"It's not too *va-va-voom*?" she asks.

"Well, there's, uh, plenty of *va* and plenty of *voom*, but it . . ."

"Yeah?"

"It's perfect."

"So, I don't look like a two-bit hooker?"

"No, no. Ten bits, at least."

She smacks my arm, and I'm suddenly very thankful it's December and I'm wearing long sleeves so she won't see how tense I am.

"I was going to try the other one on for you—it's a big, poofy red dress that looks like something Holiday Barbie would wear, but if this dress is getting *that* big of a reaction—" She shakes her head. "Anyway. Do you think he'll like it?"

"Who?"

I'm having trouble following what she's saying. My head is foggy, and my blood's pulsing in my ears and I'm trying so hard not to look at her too much, and it's basically taking everything I have in me not to confess my love for her right here, in Riddle's Bridal, surrounded by wedding dresses and two eavesdropping store clerks.

"Jeremy," she says. "Do you think he'll like it?"

The name of my best friend on her lips slaps me across the face. I cough to hide the wince, turning away from her, and then, finally, I get it. I don't know why it took me so long, but out of nowhere comes this understanding of my purpose in Sarah's life. Jeremy is her knight in shining armor, her future husband, her soul mate. I'm the court jester, the lovesick puppy, the eternal best friend, kept around because I make her laugh and feel good about herself, and all the while I feel like crap because of it.

"Graham?" She steps closer to me. "Are you okay?"

"No." The word slips out even as I tell myself to lie. But I'm tired of lying. Tired of wanting a girl who doesn't want me back.

"No," I say. "I'm not okay."

She glances around at the other women in the store, then lowers her voice. "Let me just change out of this, and then we can go outside and talk, okay? I don't have to meet Jeremy for half an hour."

Lie. Tell her you don't need to talk to her. Tell her you're not okay because you forgot your homework at school or because you've been fired from Aunt Bee's or because you hate Christmas or anything, so long as you don't tell her you've been in love with her for the past ten years and say a million other things you might regret.

But when I open my mouth, all that comes out is:

"Yeah. Okay."

Sarah changes quickly, then takes the dress up to the register, asking the saleslady to hold it until she can bring her mom in tomorrow to pay for it. Then she takes my hand and leads me outside.

It's stopped raining, and the clouds are already clearing,

the moon peeking out in between them. We cross the street and climb the stairs into the white gazebo in the middle of the square, the same gazebo where we shared snacks from Williams Pharmacy and played hide and seek when we were kids. We sit on one of the bench seats, the multicolored lights dangling from the gazebo's roof dotting Sarah's cheek like stardust.

"What's wrong?" she asks, holding her ballet bag close. If I rummaged through it, I would find her practice slippers, dirty and scratched on the bottom, not the pristine ones she saves for her performances; a case of hairpins, chipped on one side from when she dropped it on the sidewalk; two chocolate chip granola bar wrappers and a wadded-up sticker from a banana (her usual afternoon snack); and a book from her favorite manga series, the majority of which I bought for her as birthday presents and Christmas presents and just-because presents, and all of which are now torn and creased and have pages falling out from being read so many times.

Sure, Jeremy's been dating her for two years, but does he really know her? Does he know she has to keep her alarm clock set at the loudest decibel ever or she'll sleep right through it? Does he know her favorite candy is Milk Duds and that she lost four wiggly baby teeth because of them, or that I was there to witness every extraction and hand her napkins she could keep the teeth in? Does he know the scar on her knee is from when she skinned it on her swing set or that I was the one who went in and found the first aid kit because her mom had been on the phone with an important overseas client and couldn't be bothered? And the thousands of other memories I've shared with her, things Jeremy couldn't possibly begin to know after only two years.

And still, I envy him because while I have memories, Jeremy has her.

I know I shouldn't say it, know there will be no going back if I do. I stare at my shoes and force myself to say, "Nothing. I'm fine," just like I've always done.

"You're not fine." She leans close, vanilla perfume wafting from the space behind her ear and into my nose. For the millionth time in my life, I wonder what it would be like to get closer, to nuzzle her neck, to run my fingers through her hair. "Tell me."

I glance at her, and even as my brain yells, *DON'T DO IT*, I open my mouth and say the one thing I can never take back.

"How much longer are you going to be with him?"

She frowns. "I don't understand—"

"Jeremy." I sound like a jerk, but I can't stop the words from coming out. They're spring-loaded. Two years of potential energy turning kinetic. "How much longer are you going to be with him?"

"I-I don't know. For a long time, I hope."

"You love him?"

She swallows. "You know I do."

I tip my head back against the bench, ice-cold raindrops soaking my neck. "What would you say if I told you I love you too?"

She hesitates. "Of course you love me, and I love you. You and Jeremy are my best friends—"

"That's not what I mean."

She takes a deep breath. Then:

"I know."

I grit my teeth. I've always *felt* like I've been obvious, but I never thought she actually *knew*. I always figured if she did, she would have said something.

My tongue feels like sandpaper. "How long have you known?"

"I had a hunch for a while. Something about the way

you look at me."

I laugh, a harsh sound. "Great."

"Graham—"

"Why didn't you say anything?"

"Because I thought you'd move on," she says. "I thought you just wanted me because Jeremy had me. You've both always been super competitive with each other."

"Wow. You think pretty highly of me, don't you?"

"Don't do that. Don't turn me into the bad guy."

I shake my head. "That's the problem, Sarah. You could *never* be the bad guy. You think I haven't tried to get over you? You think I haven't tried to just not care? If you knew, you could have backed away, given me some space, but you're always asking for my help, always saying how much you need me, how I'm your best friend and you couldn't function without me—"

"You are," she blurts out. "I couldn't."

I know I should stop, but it's like a dam has burst, and everything I've ever thought, ever felt, but bottled down tight and ignored all these years is rushing out of me, unstoppable as a flood.

"Did you like the attention? Did you like knowing I would do anything you asked of me? Did it make you feel special?"

"Stop it." She stands. "That isn't fair. I didn't do anything to deserve this."

"It may not be fair, but it's true."

"I—I have to go. Jeremy's waiting for me."

I glance over my shoulder and see Jeremy standing outside the diner, his hands in his pockets. He bounces on his feet, and while other people would probably think he's doing it to stay warm, I know it's because he's excited to see Sarah. I know the feeling all too well, which is also how I know he loves her, and suddenly I feel like the worst sort of person, trying to break up two people who

care about each other just because I can't control my own
damn feelings.

I look back at Sarah.

Her arms are crossed over her chest, blocking me out.

A headache sprouts behind my cornea. "I'm sorry. I
didn't mean—"

"You're tired. You've been working really long hours,
and I'm exhausted from practice and this—this just wasn't
the right time to talk about this. We're saying things we
don't mean, right?"

"Right." Except I did mean them. Every single word.
"Of course."

"Talk tomorrow?"

I nod.

She uncrosses her arms and gives me a wobbly smile.
"Don't worry. We're good. Everything will be fine. We'll both
laugh about this in the morning. You'll see."

"Yeah. Sure."

She hesitates a second longer, then starts toward the diner, her boots clicking down the stairs and onto the brick
pathway. I watch as she crosses the street and embraces Jeremy, a wide smile on her face. There's no hint of concern, no
worry lines etched between her brows. No one would ever
guess what just happened by looking at her.

It's obvious she's not going to tell Jeremy—probably
thinks there's no reason for this to ruin my friendship with
him too, which is sweet of her, just the sort of thing she
would do, but if she had asked me, I would have told her it's
too late for that. There's no going back. Even if Sarah could
magically forget everything I just said, I've finally admitted
the truth to myself, finally freed the monster I've kept caged
in the back of my mind ever since Jeremy started dating
her, and now it's gutted me, hollowed out my insides, and
gnawed my heart into tiny, chewed-up pieces.

I stay on the bench for a long time. Long enough to get worried texts from Mom saying I missed dinner. Long enough for the clouds to clear, revealing a patchwork of stars. Long enough for a chill to seep into my bones and make me think I'll never be warm again.

After what seems like hours, I take a deep breath, then push off the bench.

The song "All I Want for Christmas Is You" blares through the shop speakers, echoing across the trees surrounding me. My gaze catches on Sarah and Jeremy sitting in the front window of the diner, eating burgers and sharing a milkshake. I tear my eyes away from them.

A silver flash streaks across the sky.

A shooting star.

Feeling like an idiot, I close my eyes and mutter, "All I want for Christmas is Sarah Clarke."

When I open them again, the star is gone, and Sarah is still in the diner, her fingers interlaced with Jeremy's.

I kick at a loose pebble and start for home.

4

***

I can't sleep. All I keep thinking about is what a jackass I was with Sarah. I stare at my ceiling half the night, trying to figure out how to make things right. By the time I switch off my alarm at 3:50, throw on some jeans and a hoodie, and head out to deliver the paper, the best plan I've come up with involves going back in time and stopping myself from being a jerk, so yeah, those hours weren't wasted at all.

I deliver the papers in under an hour, partly because it's cold and I don't want to be out any longer than I have to be, and partly because I'm so sleep deprived, I'm terrified I'm going to drive into a mailbox if I let myself lag for even a second. I think about picking up an "I'm sorry" doughnut for Sarah on the way home, but Saturday is the one day a week she actually lets herself sleep in, and I doubt waking her would go over well after last night.

Usually I revel in knowing things like that about her, but this morning, I hate that I know her so well. I hate that I know she went to bed crying last night because of me. I hate that I know how much guilt she feels over the things I said. Hate that I know she probably didn't sleep last night either, running scene after scene of our decade-long friendship over in her mind. And yeah, okay, I don't think the things I said were entirely wrong or untrue, but that doesn't mean I had the right to say them.

Being "real" and being cruel are two completely different things.

I don't think I've ever thought so hard or so long about anything in my life, and my head is killing me by the time I get home. I rub my thumb and index finger against the bridge of my nose as I head up the stairs to my room. At least I don't have to be at work until nine. That gives me a couple hours of sleep if I can just switch off my brain long enough to manage it.

But time is seemingly irrelevant to my Christmas-obsessed mother, who has the radio blasting again at seven, which wouldn't bother me half as much if I wasn't going on barely an hour of sleep.

I slam my pillow over my ears and shout, "It's Saturday, woman!"

I don't think it's loud enough to be heard over the music, but a second later Dad opens my door. He's halfway through tucking his shirt into his pants, and his hair's sticking up like a pinecone. "You think she cares?"

"It's getting worse," I say. "I think we need to put her in a home."

"Rehab for the Criminally Early Risers?"

"For starters."

Dad nods sleepily like such a thing might actually exist, then ambles down the hall, leaving the door wide open.

I swallow an Excedrin and jump into the shower. For a while, I just stand there, letting the hot water beat down my neck. The sensory deprivation feels good. I close my eyes and see Sarah in the gazebo, hurt and confused, her arms closing her off from me, and my heart plummets into my stomach and my stomach drops to my feet and a sharp pain like an icicle stabbing my eye rockets my head back, so I twist the knob all the way to cold and grit my teeth through the pain.

I brush my teeth next and catch my reflection in the mirror. There are dark circles under my eyes, and my skin is that kind of sickly pale that makes people take a step back when they see you so you don't puke all over their shoes. I shake my head and say the same word that's been looping through my mind all night.

"Idiot."

I change into a red sweater with a dark-green button-down underneath and a pair of khakis. Aunt Bee doesn't care much what I wear at the store during the week, but for the weekend tourists, she likes to play up the holiday angle. She thought about designing a special Christmas shirt for me to wear with the bookstore logo on it, but since she's particularly drawn to anything with a light-up Rudolph nose on it, I convinced her a polished look was more suitable for a fine establishment such as her own.

She'd grinned, deepening the wrinkles around her eyes, and wagged a finger at me. "You're blowin' nothing but smoke, but dang it if you ain't a smooth talker. You ever think about law school?"

"I think about anything that will get me away from here," I told her as I stacked a recent shipment of books in the new arrivals section.

"Now, now, Christmas is a lovely place to live. A bit on the small side, but that's what makes it fun."

"If you say so."

Aunt Bee covered my hand with her own. Her pearlescent fingernail polish caught the light like ice-slicked snow.

"She's a fool."

My heart stopped. "Who?"

"Whoever's making you want to get out of this town."

No, Aunt Bee, I think now, as I lace up my boots, painfully aware of the closed curtains of Sarah's bedroom window directly across from mine. *I'm the fool.*

Not that I'll need to tell Aunt Bee that. Even though I got the impression Sarah isn't going to share what happened between us with anyone, things like this never stay secret in a small town for long. I figure everyone will know by lunchtime, which gives me a couple hours to stuff my pillowcase with some canned food and hop the first train that comes along, although with my luck it'll probably only go as far as the next town. And then not only will I be That Guy Who Couldn't Get a Date to the Winter Formal or That Guy Who Was a Total Jerk to His Best Friend, I'll be That Moron Who Couldn't Even Manage to Leave Town Right.

The music gets louder as I walk into the hall and down the staircase. I find Mom in the dining room with bolts of wrapping paper, gift boxes, and rolls of Scotch tape scattered across the table.

"Hi, honey," she says, pressing her elbow into a gold ribbon to keep it in place as she twists the center into an elaborate bow. "Off to work?"

"In a sec," I say, walking into the dining room. "Should I not be seeing this?"

"Heavens no. I've had your presents wrapped since August. These are for the toy drive next Saturday. Remember?"

"No."

"I told you yesterday."

"Okay." Now that I'm in the room I notice more bolts of wrapping paper leaning against the wall and other presents already wrapped and tied with twine. Each present has a different decorative ornament on it: boughs of holly

and sprigs of evergreen needles, Santa-shaped cookie cut-
ters and giant candy canes. "Don't you think you're going
a little overboard?"

Mom replaces her elbow with her foot as she wrestles
the giant bow, which has a million different curls looping
through it and looks so impossibly complicated, it makes
my head hurt even worse. "Every year . . . everyone talks
about . . . what a beautiful job . . . Ruth Sayer does . . . on
her wrapping," Mom says between huge gasps for breath,
pulling the ribbon to within an inch of its life. "But this
year—*this year*—they'll be talking about . . . Martha . . .
Wallace!" She finishes tying the bow and lifts it up. "What
do you think?"

"There's some blood on the corner."

"Must have gotten a paper cut." She licks her finger and
buffs it out. "All better."

"I'm worried about you, Mom."

"Don't be," she says. "Sarah's a big help."

I freeze.

"Sarah?"

She nods.

"Sarah Clarke?" I ask.

"You have any other girlfriends named Sarah I should
know about?"

"I must have water in my ears because it sounded like you
just called Sarah Clarke my girlfriend."

"Um, yeah. I did."

"What are you talking about?"

"Are you feeling all right? You don't look so great." She
moves around the table and puts her hand on my forehead.
"Maybe you should call in sick."

I push her hand away. "I'm not sick, I'm just"—I take a
deep breath—"Mom. You know Sarah's not my girlfriend,
right?"

She crosses her arms. "Oh really? So, I've just imagined the two of you spending every waking moment together for the past two years?"

"What? We haven't—I mean, we hang out a lot yeah, but she's dating Jeremy."

"If she was dating Jeremy," Mom says, "then she'd be in *Jeremy's* kitchen making a pot of coffee right now, wouldn't she be?"

I grip the top of the dining room chair in front of me. "She's here? *Now?*"

"She promised to help me wrap these presents, remember? Over dinner last night? I didn't think you'd mind me stealing her for the day since you'd be at the bookstore."

None of this is making any sense, and my headache has officially spread down my neck and into my spine. I pinch the bridge of my nose. "Why would she be over here? We had a huge fight last night."

Mom's only half-listening now, already digging through her boxes of decorations for the next gift. "Maybe she wants to apologize."

"She's not the one who needs to apologize," I murmur, so soft I don't think Mom will hear.

She pops her head out of the box. "Maybe *you* should apologize then."

"I was planning on it as soon as I figure out what to say." A cupboard closes in the kitchen. I whip my head toward the sound, then drop my voice to a whisper. "She's *here?*"

Mom's eyes widen like she can't believe her son could be this thick.

The kitchen door swings open, and everything—my body, my heart, my ability to form a single coherent thought—slams to a halt. Sarah's hair is down and straight this morning, and she's wearing a big black cable-knit sweater over skinny jeans that are so tight they're practically illegal in thirty-nine states. She has two cups of coffee in her hands, and when she looks up at me, she smiles.

"Hey, you," she says, handing a mug to Mom but keeping her eyes on me. "You're up early. Want some coffee?"

I search her face for a single sign of anger or pain or even the slightest hint of annoyance, but there's nothing. She looks as happy and carefree as always. "You're not— you're not mad at me anymore?"

She blinks. "Why would I be mad?"

"Great," I say, lacing my fingers behind my head. "Either you two are playing a joke on me that's not funny at all, or I'm officially losing it."

Sarah's brow furrows. "You feeling okay, babe? You look really pale." She starts toward me, reaching for my forehead, but I sidestep her.

"Someone better tell me what the hell is going on."

Sarah blinks. "I'm helping your mom with the toy drive."

"I can see that, but—" I glance at Mom, then pull Sarah into the entryway and lower my voice. "What about last night?"

She looks amused now. "What *about* last night?"

"Are you trying to give me an aneurysm?"

"Oh! You mean that little fight we had?"

"*Little?*"

She cups my face in her hands. "I already told you. I don't care what movie we see tonight. All that matters is that I'm with you."

"Sarah—"

She stands on her tiptoes and presses her lips to mine. She tastes like coffee and peppermint candy. I stand rigid, so shocked at what's happening that I don't even think about putting my arms around her or deepening the kiss or doing anything else that would remotely resemble enjoying the moment I've been waiting for my entire life.

She pulls away but only slightly, her arms still hooked around my neck. "Better?"

I swallow. "What about Jeremy?"

"He can tag along tonight if he wants. I don't mind."

I shake my head. "That's not what I—"

"Sarah?" Mom calls. "Could you help me? This box doesn't want to close."

"Coming." She taps my nose before heading back into the dining room.

I've lost it. I've officially and utterly *lost* it.

I sit on the bottom step of the staircase, racking my brain. Is it the sleep deprivation? Or short-term memory loss? Did Sarah really come over last night and have dinner with us and, I don't know, announce her undying love for me?

Not only does that not make any sense, considering I know for a fact I heated up leftovers when I got home, took two bites, then threw the rest in the trash and proceeded to spend the entire night staring at my ceiling and feeling like a worthless loser, but even if Sarah and I did make up last night and we are dating now, why would she say Jeremy could come to the movies tonight? Wouldn't she want us to hide our newfound happiness instead of flaunting it in his heartbroken face? Sure, I accused her of being insensitive last night, but she isn't cruel.

And that's when I see them. The picture frames on the entryway table.

Now, I know what's *supposed* to be on that table. I've asked Mom to take down my school pictures for years, especially the ones from middle school, when I looked so awkward I would've been better off wearing a paper bag over my head. Interspersed through my school pictures should be pictures of Mom and Dad's wedding; me as a fat, wrinkly baby; and a picture from our one-and-only trip to Mexico, in which I'm sporting a wicked sunburn and thick braces.

Some of these pictures are still there, but others are gone, replaced by pictures of me with Sarah, including one from Winter Formal last year (the one I didn't attend because I had bronchitis). I'm wearing a tux and Sarah's wearing a flowy, pale pink dress that makes her look like an angel. Feeling numb from the waist down, I struggle to stand and cross to the table, taking the frame in my hands and rubbing my thumb over the glass.

Either I'm having a complete breakdown, or this picture is real.

I grab each picture in turn, testing their weight in my hands, just barely resisting the urge to throw them to the floor and see if they'll smash or maybe disappear in wisps of smoke. There's Sarah and me sitting on the couch in the family room last Christmas, our sock feet intertwined, each of us holding a mug of hot chocolate as Mom grabs a present from under the tree. Sarah and me at the Fourth of July town picnic, sitting under the same oak tree she sat underneath with Jeremy, only Jeremy isn't in the picture, and it's *my* arm around her shoulders. Sarah and me grabbing dinner after her spring recital last year, a dinner at which I remember sitting directly across from her with my hands curled into fists as she and Jeremy replayed *Lady and the Tramp* with their spaghetti. But in this picture, I'm sitting next to her and Jeremy is nowhere to be seen.

And then it hits me—*the wish*—and the picture drops from my hands, clattering against the table. "No. Freaking. Way."

"Everything all right in there, Graham?" Mom calls from the dining room.

"Y-yeah," I croak. "I think so. I'm, uh, I'm gonna go now."

"Don't forget to look up movie times," Sarah says, her voice slightly muffled by the swipe of scissors through wrapping paper.

"I won't," I call back. I stand there a moment longer, then wipe my clammy hands on my pants, grab my coat from the rack, and head out the door.

My mind is a complete blank as I walk, and I only vaguely register that the air is unusually warm for December. I don't even notice I'm sweating until I'm a block away from the bookstore, and I don't even notice I'm a block away from the bookstore until I enter the throng of weekend tourists and I'm forced to stop and swerve around large shopping bags and slow walkers.

"Graham!"

The voice comes from somewhere to my left. I look over my shoulder at Williams Pharmacy and the buff guy striding out the front door who looks, oddly, like Jeremy.

"Hey, man. What's up?" the guy asks, somehow sounding like him too.

I blink. "Jeremy?"

His brow arches. "Yeah?"

Okay, stay cool. If he wanted to punch your lights out for stealing his girl, he would have done it already. "Just, uh, heading to work. What about you? Are you . . . okay?"

He frowns. "Yeah. Why wouldn't I be?"

I lean in closer, looking for any sign of distress or heartache, but there's nothing.

"Have you been going to the gym?" I ask, flabbergasted.

Jeremy would never waste his time working out. For one, he doesn't have to. He's naturally skinny to the point of perpetual gawkiness, no matter how much junk food he eats. For another, he spends all of his spare time either playing video games, hanging out with Sarah, or playing video games *with* Sarah.

Except . . . if Sarah's my girlfriend now, and she has been for the past two years, then none of that would have ever happened.

I scan his larger frame—he even has those weird muscles on either side of his neck that make it look like someone stuffed tennis balls underneath his skin—and I wonder just how much something like this would have changed Jeremy. Sure, he was in love with Sarah, but her presence in his life couldn't have had *that* much of an effect on him.

Could it have?

"Yeah, Coach wants me to add another ten pounds and bump me up a weight class. Why? Am I starting to look freakish?"

Coach? "Are you a . . . wrestler now?"

Jeremy chuckles. "I know I'm not the best on the team, but ouch, man. That hurts."

"When did you, uh—I mean, how long have you been wrestling?"

He stops laughing. "Seriously? You should know. You were the one who convinced me to join the team in the first place."

"I was?"

"You feeling okay? You look awful."

"Yeah, I've been getting a lot of that today. Humor me, will you?"

Jeremy twists the plastic shopping bag in his hand around as he thinks. "Well, I joined the team a couple weeks into freshman year, so I guess it's a little over two years now. Why?"

Think of something that won't make you out to be more of a spaz than you already are. "I was just thinking that it's, um, about time Coach realized you belong in the higher weight class. You've been killing it out there."

I must have said something right because he's smiling again and he no longer looks like he's thinking about calling an ambulance for me. "Thanks, man. Look, I've gotta run. My little sis has a cold, and we ran out of tissues this morning. If I don't get back before she starts using the cat to wipe her nose again, Mom's gonna kill me. Want to hang out later?"

"Oh, um, Sarah and I are going to the movies."

"Oh, yeah, sure. Maybe some other time—"

"Why don't you come?"

What the hell is wrong with me? Tonight will be the first time I've *ever* been alone with Sarah as her boyfriend, and I'm inviting my best friend to tag along? But I can't take the guilt, knowing I took her away from him, even though here, in this reality, he never had her to begin with.

"Yeah, okay," he says. "I'll see you there. Text me the movie time."

I watch him disappear into the crowd, marveling at the difference in his gait and posture. When he was skinny, he loped along, arms swinging wide, a little skip in his step that made you wonder if he was perpetually on the verge of tripping or just really, really happy. Now, he walks slower, his shoulders hunched, his head tucked down, like he's walking against a windstorm no one else can feel.

You're reading too much into it. Jeremy can't miss something he doesn't know he had.

I hurry to the bookstore. There are already a couple of people waiting on the benches out front, so I head into the alley between the bookstore and the bakery and slide through the backdoor. Aunt Bee's standing in the travel section with her clipboard in hand, checking inventory. We have an electronic cash register and a huge old computer that still runs Windows '95 but when it comes to everything else, the inventory and the bookkeeping and the orders, Aunt Bee likes to do things the even more old-fashioned way: with pen and paper.

The door clicks shut behind me, and Aunt Bee turns, the Christmas lights running along the tops of the bookcases splotching her white hair with patches of red and green. She's wearing a headband with antlers and a red sweater with a cartoon scene of Santa's workshop on it.

"Hold it right there," she says.

I stop. "Sorry I'm late—"

"Oh, pish posh. You're never late. You're just running a bit slower than usual this morning." She sets down her clipboard and crosses to the register, pulling out a red Santa hat with the bookstore logo on it. "For you."

"Wow," I say, forcing a smile. "Thanks."

"Don't thank me. You'll be the laughingstock of your school if anyone sees you in it, but the customers want what the customers want, and they want everything in this town to be Christmas Christmas Christmas all the ever-loving time."

"I thought you liked that about this town," I say, tugging the hat on and moving behind the register.

"Oh, I do," Aunt Bee says. "Doesn't mean I don't recognize how those sorts of expectations can put us locals through our paces. Speaking of, business almost doubled these past two weeks from this time last year."

I'm not surprised. Our town was featured on a travel show last spring that re-aired on Thanksgiving. It doesn't hurt that we aren't far from Colonial Williamsburg either. "That's great."

"It's more than great. I've decided to give you a raise for all of your hard work. Two bucks more an hour."

"Wow, Aunt Bee. I don't know what to say."

"A thank you would be nice." She puts her hand on her hip and winks.

"Thank you."

"And that's not all. I've decided it's time to bring on another person to help out around here. I'm getting old, you know. My bones don't work like they used to."

"Really, Aunt Bee? You don't look a day over thirty."

"Aren't you sweet? I knew I kept you around for a reason."

"So, who's the new guy?" I ask, opening a box of freshly shipped books.

"New girl, actually," says a voice behind me.

Piper Hudson.

Her blonde hair is pulled back into a ponytail, and it seems Aunt Bee already gave her the memo about the holiday uniform. She's wearing a dark-green sweater with a Christmas tree pendant, a red-and-green plaid skirt, and black boots with tall, impossibly thin heels. Barely any skin is showing—just her knees, hands, neck, and face— and yet something about it feels entirely too risqué for a small-town bookstore.

I glance at Aunt Bee, certain she'll feel the same way.

Instead, Aunt Bee claps her hands and says, "Oh, don't you look darling?"

She looks like Santa's daughter, if Santa's daughter went to private school during the week and rock concerts on the weekends. The kind of girl that makes a guy bow down and say, "We're not worthy."

But Piper's not like that. She's high school cheer rallies and jasmine perfume and the creak of new book binding, and suddenly I have to fight the urge to shout at her to change before she gives some guy—the kind of guy who would think he's not only *worthy* but that he somehow deserves the right to use and abuse her until he's done with her—the wrong idea.

And next thing I know, the word "Pants" pole-vaults out of my mouth.

Piper and Aunt Bee stare at me like I've grown a second head.

"What did you just say?" Piper asks.

"Uh . . ." I scratch the back of my neck, my typical

quick-thinking gesture. Sarah would call me on it right away. Thankfully, Piper doesn't know me that well. "You might want to wear pants next time. It gets cold in here, what with the door opening and closing. And opening. And closing. You know."

Good. Smooth.

Piper blinks. "Are you feeling all right?"

"Why does everyone keep asking me that?"

Something in Aunt Bee's eyes twinkles. Her mouth quirks up into a knowing smile, and it takes me all of two seconds to decide I don't like that look.

"Piper," she says, even though she's staring at me, "why don't you observe Graham behind the register this morning, and then this afternoon you can give it a whirl while Graham supervises. Have you ever worked a register before?"

"I had a summer job at a clothing boutique back in Philly," she says, eying the out-of-date machine.

"Perfect," says Aunt Bee, who's already returned to her clipboard. "Shouldn't take you too long to get the hang of things. We open in ten minutes. Graham, why don't you run her through the basics?"

The "basics" doesn't include much since Piper's already used to the layout of the store and has some sales experience, and we're behind the counter with two minutes to spare.

"I know this beast looks terrifying," I say, gesturing to the old register, "but it's easy once you get the hang of it."

She arches a brow. "It's ancient."

I nod. "Been here since the store first opened in 'eighty-one. Aunt Bee doesn't see much point in wasting money on new equipment when the old stuff works just fine." But Piper still looks doubtful, so I add, "Just watch me for a while. Things should slow down around lunchtime, and I'll give you a proper lesson then."

"Okay," she says, taking a seat on the stool as Aunt Bee

flips the sign on the door to *OPEN* and lets in the first Christmas-shopping mob of the day.

I feel Piper's eyes on me throughout the morning. The hairs on my knuckles stand on end as she watches my fingers fly over the cash register. She leans in to ask questions, and her breath fans across my cheek and softly ruffles my hair, spreading goosebumps down my neck. At a quarter to eleven, her stomach rumbles and her lips twist up like a shrug. I tell her she can take one of the candy canes from the miniature tree on the counter, but that turns out to be a mistake because now the college-age guys in the horror section can't stop staring at her lips.

"You gonna buy something?" I shout at them before I can stop myself. "Or are you just going to ogle her all day?"

Two of them redden instantly and start combing through the books again, but the third, a tall guy with Shawn Mendes hair, smirks and makes his way toward us.

"You her boyfriend?" he asks me.

"No," I say. "But we've got a lot of customers, and if you aren't going to buy anything, you're just turning this store into a fire hazard for no reason." I gesture at the other customers, but now that it's almost lunchtime, the crowd's thinned out and there are only three other people in the store.

"Is that right?" he asks, scanning the empty aisles.

"Yeah," I lie.

He grabs a bookmark with golden retriever puppies frolicking in a wheelbarrow on it and flings it at me. Then he leans against the counter and focuses on Piper. "Hey."

"Hey," she says.

"I'm Jordan."

"Piper."

"You work here?"

"No, she just likes the high-pitched sounds the register makes," I murmur as I ring up the bookmark.

"Yes," Piper says, rolling her eyes at me. "I work here. Can I help you find something?"

"Your number?"

Is this guy serious? No way a line like that's gonna work.

"I'm not in the habit of giving guys I don't know my number," Piper says.

HA!

"That'll be a buck fifty," I tell him.

"Well then, why don't you *get* to know me?" he asks Piper, ignoring me as he pushes a dollar fifty exactly across the counter. "When do you get off work?"

"I don't know." Piper glances at me.

I hesitate. I'm not sure if she wants me to tell him the truth or if she wants me to lie and save her from him. But since they're both staring at me, waiting for an answer, I sigh and mumble, "Seven."

Jordan crosses his arms on top of the counter. "How about I take you across the street to get some coffee when you're done?"

She stares at me a moment longer, then shrugs.

"Yeah," she tells him, and my mouth drops. "Okay."

He winks. "See you at seven."

He starts to walk away. I jingle his tiny shopping bag at him. "Don't forget your bookmark."

"Keep it, Preppy," he says as he and his friends make their way toward the door. "Consider it a gift."

Preppy?

I turn to Piper. "I don't look preppy, do I?"

She takes in my button-down shirt and sweater combo. "You look professional."

"You didn't answer the question."

"It's not a question I feel like answering."

"I think you just did."

"You realize you're talking to a cheerleader, right? I'm not exactly in the camp that thinks being preppy's a bad thing."

Crap, did I offend her again? Or is this the first time I've offended her? I guess our conversation about the winter formal yesterday wouldn't have happened if I've been dating Sarah for two years, but that's not to say I haven't offended Piper over something else in this alternate life.

This is getting confusing.

Another customer comes forward with three books and a magazine. I ring her up, and we make small talk about the weather. Once she's gone, I wipe imaginary dust off the counter and ask, "Are you into that guy?"

"Is it really any of your business?" Piper's smiling like she's teasing, but there's an edge to her words that feels like a dare.

"I guess not." I hesitate. "It's just—I don't want to see you get hurt."

"Excuse me?"

"Come on, you know how guys are, especially guys like him. They see a girl in a skirt and boots, and suddenly they lose all brain function."

"Ah. The 'pants' comment."

"Guys like that only want one thing."

"I'll keep that in mind, *Grandpa*," she says, crossing her arms. "And for your information, I shouldn't have to give up wearing skirts and boots that I like just because guys like *you* will use it as an excuse to be a complete moron. And furthermore, I'm sitting behind a counter, knucklehead. He couldn't even see anything below my waist. Here's a thought: maybe, just *maybe*, he was attracted to me for some other reason."

"Did you just call me a knucklehead?"

"Is that really all you got from what I just said?"

"Yeah. No one's used that word since 'fifty-six."

She smirks even though I can tell she's trying to fight

it. "It's one of Queenie's favorite words. She has her own special brand of cursing."

"Queenie?"

"My grandma," she explains. "When I was born, she decided she was too cool to be a Grandma. So, she's Queenie."

"You spend a lot of time with your grandma?"

She gives me an odd look. "I live with her."

"Oh."

Was I supposed to know that already? I decide to take the chance that if I didn't know that about her in my previous, dateless life (especially when I had so much free time to ask), there's a good chance I wouldn't know it now either, when presumably the majority of my time outside of work and school has been taken up by Sarah.

Piper sighs. "Go ahead."

"'Go ahead' what?"

"I know you want to ask where my parents are."

"No," I say quickly.

She arches a brow.

"Okay. Maybe a little."

"It's okay," she says. "Everyone asks—or wants to ask, and you don't have to worry. They're not dead or anything. They're just . . . dead to each other."

"Divorce?"

"A pretty bad one. They're both lawyers, so they know how to drag it out long enough to make it really hurt."

"Sorry. That sucks."

"It's not a big deal, especially now that I've gotten away from it. I'm just happy Queenie was willing to take me in. It was supposed to be just a couple weeks at the end of the summer, but my parents are stubborn, and neither of them wants to give the other what they want, so there's a good chance they'll still be getting divorced when I start college." She runs her fingers over the rolls of orange *SALE* stamps

Aunt Bee keeps stashed behind the counter. "What about you? Parents still together?"

"Yep. Twenty years and counting."

"You're lucky," she whispers.

I open my mouth to say something, even though I have no clue what to say to fix the pain in Piper's eyes, but Aunt Bee drops a stack of order forms on the counter and says, "Lunchtime. Take five, kids. I'll man the register."

Piper slips off her stool and moves around me. I start for the staff room, but Aunt Bee says, "Graham?"

"Yeah?"

"Next time you want to harass a group of customers for staring at Piper—don't, okay?"

I give her a sheepish smile. "Sorry."

She glances over my shoulder, then drops her voice to a whisper. "What's up with the two of you? I thought you were practically married to that Clarke girl."

"I am?" I grin. "I mean . . . yeah, I am. I just—I don't know. I guess I wanted to protect her."

"*Mm-hmm*. Well, don't let it affect your work, or else I'll be taking that raise back and then some. The last thing I need in my life is a bunch of teenage drama. I didn't appreciate it when *I* was in high school, and I certainly don't appreciate it now."

"Yes, ma'am."

***

After lunch, Piper takes over the register while Aunt Bee sets me up front in the display window, stacking books in a spiral to look like a Christmas tree. Piper calls me after hitting a wrong button and then again after wrestling with the drawer when it refuses to open, but she gets the hang of it after that. By mid-afternoon, I'm able to

take care of the orders for next week, a task I usually have
to stay late for, and I have to admit, having a coworker is
working out even better than I thought it would.

Foot traffic starts to slow down at half past six, so I look up
movie times and send them to Sarah and Jeremy. We decide
on an eight-thirty showing, giving me enough time to head
home and change into something less "yuletide carols."

Jeremy texts: You sure it's okay I tag along? I don't want to
be a third wheel.

I reply: Already cleared it with Sarah. You're coming.

But he's got a point. I'm completely new at this whole
"dating Sarah" thing, and I don't want to spend my entire
night wondering whether Jeremy's about to remember I
stole his girl and punch my lights out.

I glance at Piper using the camera on her phone to re-
apply her lip gloss, and I have to force myself not to roll
my eyes.

"Going to a lot of trouble for a guy you just met."

"Do you hear that?" Piper asks, not looking at me. "It
sounds like someone's trying to talk to me, but all I hear is
blah blah blah—"

"Very mature. All I'm saying is you could do better than
that guy."

"Got someone in mind?"

My phone buzzes. Jeremy replying with a simple: K.

"Actually . . ." I tap my phone against the counter and
plaster on my most convincing smile. "How do you feel
about meeting me and some friends at the movies after your
little coffee thing?"

She frowns. "Like a . . . date?"

"Yeah, kind of."

"I thought you were dating Sarah Clarke."

"I am. I meant a date with my friend. Jeremy Davis?"

She blushes. "Oh."

"You really didn't think I meant me, did you?"

I barely even had the courage to ask her out when she was practically my only option to go to the winter formal. No way I'd ask her out now, when I'd be risking my relationship with Sarah, a relationship begotten off a shooting star, no less—which means if I find some way to screw it up, I'll have changed my entire life and the lives of the people around me for no reason at all.

"No, of course not," she says quickly. "I just didn't know who you meant."

"So? How about it?"

She chews her bottom lip. "Sure. Why not?"

"Great."

I flip out my phone and text Jeremy, letting him know I've set him up with somebody.

He doesn't respond.

A minute later, the Shawn Mendes wannabe shows up outside the display window, tapping his knuckles on the glass.

"Prince Charming has arrived," I mutter.

Piper checks her watch. "He's six minutes early."

"Go ahead," I say. "I'll lock up."

"You sure?"

Not really. I don't know what it is about this guy, but I don't want Piper going out with him. Still, even when I want to be a jerk, I can't seem to let the nice guy act slide. I blame my mother.

"No problem," I tell her. "But don't get too attached. You'll be kicking that guy to the curb as soon as you meet Jeremy."

"I'll keep that in mind."

She ducks out of the store. Jordan puts his arm around her, his fingertips hanging precariously close to her chest as he leads her across the street. I grind my teeth and force my gaze away.

It doesn't really hit me until I've locked up the store and started for home, passing the same white gazebo I sat in last night, when I thought I had lost Sarah forever, that tonight, Sarah's waiting for me.

Not Jeremy.

Me.

And despite all the guilt and confusion and downright certainty that I did nothing to deserve this, I couldn't be happier.

5

***

Sarah has ballet practice until eight, so we decide to meet at the theater. It takes me thirty minutes to decide what to wear, which makes me feel like I'm in one of those '80s movie montages where I can't pick the right outfit to save my life, but this is my first official date with Sarah Clarke and I want to make a good impression (even though I tell myself I must have made a good impression two years ago or she wouldn't still be dating me).

A short, chilly walk later, I enter the foyer of the old-fashioned two-screen movie theater off of Front Street, wondering if three dabs of cologne was too much and running my hand across my face to check for the thousandth time if I missed any patches while shaving.

I spot her by the ticket booth. Her hair is swept to one side, curly from being up in her ballerina bun, and she's wearing dark leggings and a big gray sweater that hangs off her shoulder. My heart thumps against my ribcage as her eyes meet mine, and her face breaks into a smile that, just yesterday, had been reserved for Jeremy.

The rest of the theater melts into a blur as she glides toward me, her ballet bag swinging at her side. She wraps her arms around my neck. "Hey, you."

And then she kisses me, her lips dancing across mine. It's an unfamiliar, slightly awkward feeling, like puzzle pieces that don't quite fit, and yet nothing in my life has ever felt so right as holding her in my arms.

She pulls away first and stares up at me from beneath her lashes.

"Hey," I say back. The word comes out breathy, and she giggles.

"Like what you see?"

I nod, not trusting myself to speak.

Someone clears their throat loudly behind Sarah.

Jeremy.

"What's up?" he asks, his hands in his pockets, his shoulders curved like they were earlier today, as if eternally stuck mid-shrug.

"Not much," Sarah says, threading her fingers through mine.

"How was practice?" Jeremy asks her.

"Fine, although Madame still hasn't decided between me and Lindsay for the lead."

"What? But you're always Clara!" Jeremy sputters. "It wouldn't be *The Nutcracker* if you weren't."

Sarah gives him a half smile. "Thanks, but that's kind of the problem. Madame wants the other girls to step it up. She thinks if the roles are always going to me, they won't have the drive to compete for them."

Jeremy's brow furrows. "That doesn't make any sense. That should make them want to work harder."

Sarah shrugs. "It doesn't really matter, so long as I'm good enough to get into Juilliard. I can't believe I'll be applying a year from now."

I frown. "Juilliard?"

Sarah glances at me. "Yeah?"

"Since when are you going to Juilliard?"

"Oh, ha ha, very funny."

"I'm serious," I say. "I thought you wanted to go to William & Mary. Be closer to home."

"No," Sarah says, drawing out the word into three syllables. "I'm going to Juilliard and you're going to NYU, remember? We talked about it last Christmas."

"But—"

And then it hits me. She wanted to go to William & Mary when she was dating Jeremy. They dreamt of being townies together for the rest of their lives. Sarah talked about possibly taking over the dance studio when Madame Dufort retires, and she and Jeremy were going to raise little Christmas-loving, ballet-dancing, Cheeto-finger babies together. But I've never wanted that. My plan has always been to leave, go somewhere big and loud where I can get lost in a surge of people. I always thought I wanted that to get away from Sarah, to meet new people and finally move on. I never thought I would have wanted that if Sarah and I were together.

Sure, I love my hometown, but now that I think about it, I guess I've always felt … I don't know … too big for it. And now that Sarah's with me, it seems her dreams have gotten bigger too. But is Juilliard really what she wants? Or does she just want to be where I am?

Who's the real Sarah? The one standing here with me, dreaming of a ballet career in a big city, or the one who fell in love with Jeremy, who wanted nothing more than to drive a minivan and stay in Christmas, Virginia the rest of her life? Has dating me completely ruined her life, or have I set her free to finally go after what she really wants?

I'm so wrapped up in my thoughts, I don't even realize Piper has shown up until she sticks her hand out to Jeremy and says, "Well, since the guy who invited me won't introduce us, I guess I'll do it. I'm Piper."

Jeremy takes her hand. "Jeremy."

"We should really get in there," Sarah says, tugging me forward. "I don't want to miss the previews."

We grab our tickets and head for the concession stand. Jeremy buys two soft drinks and an extra-large popcorn for him and Piper to share.

"What are you thinking?" I ask Sarah as Jeremy digs through his jeans for his wallet. "Two Cokes, large popcorn, and some Milk Duds?"

"Only if you're that hungry."

"Oh yeah, like you're not going to help me. I've watched you ravage an all-you-can-eat buffet after one of your practices before."

Sarah's mouth drops. "You have not!"

"The other customers had to wait for the kitchen to restock half the food."

"I'm drinking protein shakes after practice now, remember?" She opens her bag to reveal a plastic bottle filled with a gray, chunky liquid.

"Yeah," I say. "Looks real appetizing."

She smacks my arm.

"Okay . . . just Milk Duds, then?"

She shakes her head. "How do you expect me to get into Juilliard if I'm stuffing my face full of pointless calories all the time?"

"But they're your favorite pointless calories."

"Graham. My professional ballet career will last five years—ten if I'm lucky. I can eat all the Milk Duds I want when I retire, but until then, I'm sticking to my nutritionist's diet."

"But—"

She shoots me a glare, so I keep my mouth shut.

Jeremy and Piper move aside, Jeremy already throwing pieces of popcorn into the air and swerving to catch them on his tongue. A popcorn kernel bounces off his nose, and Piper laughs.

I sigh, grab a small Coke and a hot dog, and follow them into the theater.

✳✳✳

It's an odd feeling, trying to get used to this new Sarah. I try not to let it bother me. It makes sense that she would have changed a little, having spent the last two years with me instead of Jeremy, and if something as big as her life's ambition really has changed, then naturally a few smaller things would have changed too. So what if she doesn't eat Milk Duds anymore? She's still Sarah Clarke—still perfection personified. And when she holds onto my arm throughout the movie, her thumb rubbing absently up and down my ribcage, it becomes difficult to think of anything at all, which becomes evident when we leave the theater and Sarah asks, "So, what'd you think?"

"Oh. Uh. Pretty funny."

Her eyes narrow. "It was a crime drama."

"Oh yeah. I just meant that one part, you know, was funny. Hey guys," I say, turning to Piper and Jeremy, "want to grab some ice cream?"

"Sure," Piper says. "I've already eaten my weight in popcorn and downed a thousand calories in cappuccinos, so why not?"

"I can't," Sarah says. "Diet, remember?"

"Oh."

"Yeah, I can't either," Jeremy says.

"I thought you were trying to put on weight?" I ask him.

"Well, yeah." He digs his hands into his pockets. "But it needs to be the right kind of food, and I've already butchered my diet tonight with that popcorn. If you two want to get some ice cream"—he gestures to Piper and me—"I could walk Sarah home. I mean, since it's on the way—"

"No," I say quickly. "I'll walk her home. I do live right next door."

"I don't mind—" Sarah starts to say, but I wave off her comment and turn to Piper.

"Another time?" I ask her.

"Yeah, sure," Piper says.

I put my arm around Sarah and ease her away from Jeremy, suddenly terrified that their close proximity will somehow spark memories of our pre-wish lives. "Why don't you walk Piper home, Jer?"

He shrugs.

"That's okay," Piper says. "I don't live far from here."

"No, it's fine," Jeremy says, but his voice is low and unconvincing, and Piper gives me a look that says: *Bookstore Boy's looking better by the minute.*

We say our goodbyes—Jeremy acting surlier than I've ever seen him—and I walk Sarah home, her hand cupping mine.

"Is everything okay with Jer?" I ask her.

"I think so," she says. "Why?"

"Nothing. He just seems . . . different."

"I haven't noticed."

My palm starts to sweat from the heat of hers, and I move to pull my hand away, but she holds on tighter, and I think, *This is how it feels to have Sarah Clarke love you back.*

My thoughts of Jeremy slip away, and I smile down at her. "You know something?"

"What?"

"I love you."

My breath catches in my throat as I wait for her response, certain this has all been a mistake, a dream. That I'll wake up any second now and things will go back the way they were.

She smirks and kisses the back of my hand. "I love you too, even when you're trying to sabotage my diet."

"I won't anymore. Promise."

Because all that matters now is that I have her, the girl I've been dreaming about since she moved in next door a decade ago. So what if a couple things have changed? She's still the same girl. Still the only thing I've ever wanted in this world. If she wants to be a nutrition freak and a professional ballet dancer, I'm not going to stand in her way. I don't want to give her a reason to break up with me now that I have her.

I kiss her goodnight at the gate in front of her house and then head down the path to my front porch, thanking God this day turned out a million times better than I ever thought it could.

6

* * *

Over the next week, Sarah and I spend all of our free time together, watching Christmas movies next to the fireplace, doing our homework on the kitchen table while Mom makes dinner, and then helping her make a gingerbread house for the display at city hall (even Dad gets roped into that one, although he gets more icing on Mom's nose than on the house).

Business at the store picks up too, but I barely notice it now that Piper's getting the hang of things, although I have to remind her on a daily basis, as she combs through the stacks, that she'd take home a much bigger paycheck if she didn't blow half of it on the merchandise.

"You know Christmas is coming, right?" I ask her on Wednesday night as we lock up. The temperatures have been hovering in the forties, and rain trickles down the display windows. "That time of year when you should be telling people what you want instead of buying it all for yourself?"

"How could I not, living in this town?"

"Seriously. You should stop shopping and make a list."

"Queenie doesn't have a lot of money. She usually just knits me a pair of gloves or a hat or something."

"What about your parents?"

She scoffs. "The only date they have circled on their calendars is their next court hearing, also known as their next 'tell blatant lies about each other and accomplish nothing' hearing."

"Okay, then. What about me?"

She glances over her shoulder. "What about you?"

"What if I want to get you something?"

"Why would you do that?" She tries to sound nonchalant, but suspicion creeps into her voice.

"Because I want to."

"I don't want any pity gifts."

"That's good because I wasn't planning on giving you any. I was thinking more along the lines of a coworker gift. Or maybe even a 'friend' gift, although you're not winning yourself any points in that category right now, looking at me with those squinty eyes."

Her face relaxes. "Oh."

I lean against the bookcase and grab the book she's currently holding. *The Fountainhead* by Ayn Rand. "So, how about it?"

"Okay."

"Good." I take the book back to the counter and place it on the reserved shelf, ignoring her sputters of disbelief. "Then you won't see this again until Christmas."

She crosses her arms over her chest. "Well, if I already know what you're getting me, why can't I just have it now?"

"Because you don't know what I'm getting you."

"Uh, pretty sure I do."

"It's just on the reserved shelf in case I can't think of

anything else to get. Either way, you won't be buying this book today."

She rolls her eyes but can't quite hide her smile.

On Thursday, I pick Sarah up after ballet practice to go Christmas shopping for our parents. I pick up a fancy French cookbook Mom's been eyeing in the bookstore, and I get Dad a used pair of noise-cancelling headphones so he can sleep through Mom's early morning Christmas music this time next year. It isn't until our walk home, when I tell Sarah that Mom's invited her over for dinner again, that I think of something.

"Why don't we ever hang out at your house?" I ask as we pass the town square, where booths are already being set up for Saturday's annual Christmas toy drive.

"You're kidding, right?"

"Uh . . . no?"

"Come on, Graham. You know how my parents feel about you."

"Yeah. They love me."

Her brow arches.

"They *don't* love me?"

"Not really."

"But I'm a lovable guy."

"Well, *I* think so."

"Seriously. I don't drink. I don't smoke. I don't do drugs. I keep my grades up, I work hard, and—"

"And you're a great kisser."

"I am?" *Stop it, Graham. Concentrate.* "I just don't get it. We've been best friends since we were kids. They've known me almost my whole life."

"Well, that's kind of the problem, isn't it? You used to be safe, reliable Graham. Now you're the enemy."

My jaw drops. "They didn't have a problem with Jeremy, and they barely even knew him!"

She blinks. "What does Jeremy have to do with anything?"

I shove my hands into my pockets so I don't smack myself across the face.

"Never mind. Did I ... did I do something *specific* to make them hate me?"

"Well, that time they caught us making out in the basement didn't help. Oh, Graham," she says with a little chuckle at my horrified expression, wrapping her arms around my waist, "don't worry about it. I don't care what they think."

"I do."

"You never have before."

"I highly doubt that."

She smiles and tugs me forward. "Come on. Let's go to your house. I think I worked off enough calories tonight to justify some of your mom's pasta."

We start down the sidewalk, passing a Santa with a charity bucket. I fish a twenty out of my wallet and drop it into the slot.

"Ho ho ho! Merry Christmas!" Santa calls after us, but I barely hear him. The same thought keeps circling my mind: How could Mr. and Mrs. Clarke love Jeremy—chews with his mouth open, C-average, video game junkie *Jeremy*—and not me? Not that I'm without faults or anything, but there are a ton of worse guys she could be dating. Like that sleazeball Piper's seeing. They aren't officially dating, but he took her out for coffee a couple more times this week, and thinking about *that* puts me in an even fouler mood.

The thought stays with me on Saturday morning as Sarah and I walk around the booths selling hot chocolate and homemade cookies at the toy drive. Aside from the toy collection, there are booths from all the local shops as well as some local artists selling paintings, jewelry, and Christmas decorations, with fifty percent of the proceeds going to the children's hospital.

"You're thinking about it again, aren't you?" Sarah asks me as she browses a display of necklaces with stained-glass pendants.

"No," I lie.

"Well, stop it. You're being neurotic over nothing."

"Is it really such a bad thing that I want your parents to like me? If we're going to make this work—"

"What do you mean '*if* we're going to make this work?' We've been making it work for two years."

"I mean," I say, fiddling with the ornaments on the Christmas tree in the corner of the booth, "in the long run."

"In the long run, we're going to be in New York, far away from them. They might visit on some holidays and we might visit them on others, but it's not like we're going to be one big happy family living in the same town. It doesn't matter." But there's an edge to her voice as she says it, and I know it bothers her more than she's letting on. "Now can we give it a rest?"

Or maybe I'm reading too much into it. Maybe in this alternate universe, when Jeremy was never her boyfriend and I never would have known her parents had favored him over me, I really wouldn't have cared how they felt about me. Regardless, talking to Sarah about it won't change how her parents feel. If I want them to like me, I'll have to start doing things to make them like me.

"You're right," I say, putting my arm around her as we move to the next booth. "It doesn't matter. And besides, we have a year and a half before we're out of this town for good. A lot can change between now and then."

Out in the middle of the square, volunteers huddle around two dozen crates of Christmas lights, unknotting strands and laying them on long tables, with the big old-fashioned bulbs on one table, followed by modern

LEDs, icicle lights, and twinkle lights on the others. After those come ornaments of all shapes and sizes, shiny gold and silver tinsel, long strands of velvet ribbons and gigantic red bows, and old-fashioned nutcrackers and cans of spray-paint snow. As per the toy drive tradition, there's always a decorating contest of some kind in the square. Weather permitting, there'll be a snowman-building contest, but since it's been a warm, rainy December, the town council has put off decorating the various pine and oak trees surrounding the square in favor of a tree-decorating competition. I spot Mom at the entrance-fee table, designating assigned trees to each team.

"Speaking of my family," Sarah says, pointing to her mom, dad, and younger brother, David, perusing the ornaments. They don't often find time to get everyone together, the Clarke family, what with both of Sarah's parents' work schedules, Sarah's daily ballet practice, and David participating in his middle school's basketball team in the fall and track in the spring, but they sign up for this competition every year for some quality bonding time. I would know, since I helped Mom set up the event every year until I started working at the bookstore, and even then, I could see the Clarke family in the square from the store window. They used Jeremy's height to their advantage the last two years, making extra tall snowmen.

There's a thought. I may not be as tall as Jeremy, but I've been known to climb a tree or two back in my day.

I squeeze Sarah's hand. "Hey."

"Hey yourself."

"Do you think your parents would mind if I joined your team?"

Sarah groans. "Graham—"

"Come on. How are they ever going to like me if I don't show them my charming, adorable side?"

She checks her watch. "Don't you have to get back to the store soon?"

"Piper's covering until one."

"This really means a lot to you, doesn't it?"

"Yeah," I say. "It does."

"Okay, I'll go ask."

She gives me a peck on the cheek and walks off, dragging her feet slightly.

I smell her perfume first, that clean scent of jasmine and a hint of something darker, more mysterious, and then Piper comes to a stop next to me, wearing black pants, a gray sweater with white snowflakes, and an open red coat.

"Quite the shindig you've got going on here," she says, her eyes sweeping the square. "They do this every year?"

"Aren't you supposed to be at the store?"

"Aunt Bee gave me a ten-minute break when I told her I'd never been in town for the toy drive before."

"Your parents never visited your grandma this time of year?"

"Sacrilege, right? I mean, people come from all over the place to visit this town in December, but my parents have always hated crowds, so they'd buy a plane ticket for Queenie to come to us. I only ever visited her in the summer, when my parents wanted to get rid of me for a couple weeks." She gives me a sidelong look. "You don't need to stare at me like that, you know."

"Like what?"

"Like you're sorry. I don't say this stuff to make you feel bad for me. It's just the truth, and it's really not that bad in the grand scheme of things. I mean, I don't have a right to complain when you think about all the people in this world going through so much worse."

"Everyone has the right to complain. The fact that someone else is dealing with a bigger crisis in another part of the world doesn't make you feel any less hurt when your parents want to get rid of you."

"You talk about it like you've experienced it."

"Not on the parent front," I say. "If anything, they've been *too* clingy over the years." I glance at Sarah. "But I do know what it feels like to be cast aside."

She takes a deep breath. "Yeah, well, that's enough depressing talk for one day. Are you decorating a tree?"

I watch Sarah speaking to her parents with what seems like way too many hand gestures. Her parents exchange frowns.

"That remains to be seen," I say.

Jeremy's watching her too, although he's trying to hide it, leaning up against a tree with a foam cup and a coffee straw he keeps twirling, looking up from underneath his brow every few seconds. I want to ignore him more than anything. Want to tell myself that he doesn't have feelings for Sarah, that I'm reading into things that aren't really there, but I can't. Instead, I wonder if that's how I looked, loving Sarah Clarke from afar.

Did Jeremy know how I felt about her? Was I that obvious?

I turn back to Piper. "Hey, you have a date for the winter formal yet?"

She rolls her eyes. "I thought I said I was over the depressing talk."

"So, that's a no?"

"No one's asked me, and I don't expect anyone to. No one waits until a week before the dance to ask someone out."

"You'd be surprised," I mutter. "How about Jeremy?"

She gives me a half smile. "Look, Graham, I think it's really sweet that you're trying to set me up with your friend, but I don't think he's that into me."

"What? Of course he is."

"He has a funny way of showing it."

"He's just shy. I'm sure if I asked him—"

"Oh yeah because every girl wants her date to be coerced into taking her out."

"He doesn't have to be coerced into anything. It's just that you're still pretty new here, and new girls are always a little intimidating. Come on, I don't want you to be home alone on the night of the—*ow!* You hit me!"

"What did I just say about feeling bad for me? Besides, I think I might ask Jordan."

"He wouldn't be into that sort of thing," I say, rubbing my arm. "Would he?"

She shrugs. "I don't know, but it doesn't hurt to ask."

I'm trying to think of reasons why Piper shouldn't go out with him that would actually make some kind of logical sense—as opposed to the overall illogical feeling I have that the guy is just bad news—when Sarah comes bounding up to me.

"You're in," she says. "Hey, Piper."

Piper waves. "Hey."

"In what?" I ask.

"Seriously? I just spent the past five minutes begging my parents, and you've already forgotten?"

"Oh! Sorry. I got distracted."

Sarah slides a cold look Piper's way.

"Yeah, that's my fault," Piper says quickly. "I was asking him about this order form I was supposed to fill the other night. It was really complicated, and I think I might have deleted a file on that Pandora's box of a computer."

Sarah relaxes. "Oh. Everything okay now?"

"Yep. Don't know what I'd do without this guy covering for me." She laughs, and Sarah smiles up at me. "Anyway," Piper continues, "I'm just going to grab some cocoa and head back to the store. Good luck."

"Thanks," Sarah says, watching Piper go. She turns to me and takes my hands in hers. "She's really nice."

"Yeah." And a quick thinker. I would have hugged her for that if it wouldn't have roused Sarah's suspicions again. But really, how could Sarah think I'd be interested in Piper when I've been obsessed with *her* for the past ten years?

I kiss the top of her head. "You're beautiful, you know that?"

She flicks my nose. "You're not so bad yourself. Now come on. We can't start decorating the tree until the entire team gets there, and if we're dawdling all the way back here when the whistle blows, my parents will never forgive you."

"You're kidding, right?"

"Not even a little bit."

We jog to the starting line.

"Hello Mr. Clarke, Mrs. Clarke," I say, stretching my hand out, but Sarah's dad shakes his head.

"Get into your starting positions," he says, and, as one, the entire Clarke family bends over like Olympic sprinters, their fingertips pressed into the cold, damp grass. "Mom and I will go for the lights. Sarah and Graham, take the ornaments. You've got the tinsel, Davey."

"Aye, aye, sir," David says, not even a hint of sarcasm in his voice.

I'm so taken aback by their intensity that I just stand there, watching them.

"Come on, Graham. Get ready," Sarah hisses, looking over her shoulder at me.

"Oh. Right."

I bend over, mimicking their pose.

The mayor speaks into a megaphone from the edge of the starting line. "All teams will gather their supplies into their baskets and head for their designated trees, where they will have one hour to complete their decorations before judging commences. Everyone ready? On the count of three. One... two... three!"

He blows the whistle, and everyone around me takes

off like a bunch of rabid Christmas-tree-decorating fanat-
ics. I'm pretty sure the guy next to me is foaming at the
mouth, but I don't turn my head to look. The chances are
too high that I'll get trampled, and the Clarke family will
leave me to die in the middle of the square. I can just hear
Mr. Clarke now: "Your dying wasn't part of the plan, Wallace! Get it together!"

We reach the extra-large baskets and each grab one, then
head for the tables. Mr. and Mrs. Clarke are the first ones to
the lights, but Sarah, David, and I are behind a few people at
the ornaments and tinsel table. I hang back, waiting for the
group ahead of me to finish picking things over, but Sarah
elbows her way through.

"Get in here, Graham!" she shouts, scooping ornaments
into her basket.

I slide in next to her, muttering apologies to the people
around me.

"Your family's intense," I tell Sarah.

"Nothing wrong with being a little competitive. Now
move!" She shoots off, and I grab a couple handfuls of plastic ornaments in 1950s retro styles.

Piper's watching from the sidelines, her hand over her
mouth like she's trying not to laugh. She waves at me and
points to a make-believe watch on her wrist, mouthing,
"Better hurry."

I roll my eyes at her, and even though I know I shouldn't
do anything to make the Clarkes hate me even more than
they already do, I slow to a walk as I head toward our assigned pine tree. Mr. Clarke shouts at me to get my ass over
there so they can start decorating, but that just makes me
grit my teeth harder and walk slower. That is until Sarah
glares at me, and I remember that I asked for this and it isn't
her fault that I never noticed how seriously her family takes
this whole thing. I always thought they just did it for fun.

Family bonding. To get into the Christmas spirit.

You know, *normal* reasons.

I pick up the pace, and when I get to the tree, I mutter, "Sorry. Leg cramp."

But they aren't listening to me. It seems they were coming up with a game plan while I took my sweet time, and now Mr. Clarke's ordering everyone around like a drill sergeant.

"You guys know this isn't a race, right?" I ask Sarah as we help David wrap tinsel around the tree. We're circling the branches so fast I think I might puke, and I seriously regret the dozen or so cinnamon rolls I stuffed in my mouth half an hour ago.

"There's a rule that if you clear your baskets before the hour's up, you can go back for more decorations," she says. "So if you want to have the best tree, then yeah. It kind of is."

For the next hour, I bite my tongue and do what I'm told. I don't think I've ever been happier to go to the store than I am when the clock strikes one and the mayor blows his whistle and calls time.

"Everyone, drop your decorations and step away from your trees," he says. "The judges will come around now and inspect your work, but before we begin, the town council would like to remind everyone that attempts at bribery will warrant an immediate disqualification, thanks to last year's double fudge brownie debacle. Although the perpetrators swear the brownies were leftovers that needed to be eaten and not at all a bribe"—he narrows his eyes at the Clarkes, and I take another step back from them, my hands in my pockets as if I just happened to walk into their general vicinity but am not at all associated with them—"other participants felt it was entirely unfair and questioned the winning team. So, this year we ask that the participants not speak to the judges until the contest is over and the winners have been chosen."

I clear my throat. "Well, time for me to go."

"Don't you want to see who wins?" Sarah asks.

"I have to get to the store. Fill me in later?"

To be honest, I'm kind of dreading the possibility that they might lose. Sure, our tree looks like something out of a department store catalog, but there are a lot of other great trees, and I have a feeling the blame will fall on me and my dubious "leg cramp" if they don't win.

"Okay." She gives me a quick kiss. "See you later."

Jeremy catches up to me at the other end of the square. "You okay?"

"Yeah. Why?"

"You look pale."

"Just a little shell-shocked. You'd think we were going to war the way Mr. Clarke was barking at everybody. Is he like that every year?"

Jeremy frowns. "How should I know?"

"Oh right. You shouldn't." I shake my head. "You have a date to the winter formal yet?"

"I was thinking I'd skip it this year."

"Why?"

"Well." Jeremy hesitates. "It's kind of ridiculous, right?"

"That's what people who don't have dates say. Why don't you ask Piper?"

"Nah, I'm sure she's already got a date—"

"No, she doesn't. I already asked her."

"Oh. Well. I don't know."

"Come on, Jer. You can't let a high school milestone like this pass you by just because—" The words collide against my teeth. I was about to say *just because you're in love with Sarah*, but if Jeremy had said something like that to me, I would have changed my name and jumped the first train to Alaska.

"Just because," I start again, "you don't see the point of it."

Jeremy sighs. "I'll think about it."

"Good."

He nods and walks off, and I head for the bookstore, which turns out to be empty save for one customer perusing our nonfiction titles. Piper's standing behind the counter, reading a creased and earmarked copy of *Little Women*, with half the pages sticking out as if they'd fallen out of the taped-up binding years ago. She doesn't look up at the sound of the sleigh bells tinkling over the door as I walk in. In fact, the only sign that she's even remotely still aware of what's going on around her is her foot tapping to the melody of "Jingle Bell Rock" streaming through the store's hidden speakers as she writes notes in the margins of her book with a little pencil.

"Good book?" I ask.

She jumps. "Oh, hey. Yeah. I've read it a thousand times."

"I couldn't tell."

She stuffs it in her purse. "Okay if I get out of here now?"

"No problem."

She pulls on her coat and wraps her scarf around her neck. "That was some performance."

I huff out a breath. "I suppose it would be too much to ask that we not mention it ever again?"

"Way too much," she says, a wide smile dimpling her cheeks. "I've seen snails with more pep in their step."

"Yeah, well, I didn't realize the Clarkes were the Usain Bolts of tree decorating."

She cocks her head to the side. "But haven't you and Sarah been dating for a while now?"

"Two years," I manage to answer, but only because I've practiced saying it every night so that I don't accidently blurt out that we've only been dating a week, no matter what those photos on Mom's entryway table say. "But I've never been invited to join their team before this year."

"I can see why."

"Har-har."

"I'm just giving you a hard time. I would've been the same way, especially if Mr. Clarke had yelled at me like that. At least you kept walking toward them and didn't run the other way."

"Yeah, I guess."

"It explains a lot though, doesn't it? About Sarah?"

My brow furrows. "What do you mean?"

"Well, she's really into her ballet training, right? One of the girls on the squad told me she practices six days a week, more than any other student at the academy."

"She wants to be a professional ballerina. It's kind of what you have to do."

"No, I get that, but I mean ... well, she's kind of competitive in her personal life too, you know?"

"No, I don't."

She gives me a pointed look. "Come on, Graham. I saved your butt back there. I mean, you and I both know you weren't distracted *because* of me, but you saw that look Sarah gave me. It was pure jealousy."

I did see it, and I thought the same thing, but I immediately bristle at the way she's talking about Sarah. "I didn't notice."

"Really? It was pretty obvious to me—"

"Sarah isn't like that," I bite back. A small voice in the back of my mind whispers, *Who exactly are you trying to convince here?* But I shove it back to wherever it came from.

Piper holds up her hands. "Sorry. I guess I misunderstood."

"Yeah, you did."

"Okay ... well now that things are officially weird between us, I think I'll go."

I can tell she's trying to make me laugh, but I don't give

her the satisfaction.

She nods, gripping the strap of her purse tight, and turns to leave—

"Wait right there, missy," Aunt Bee says, striding out of her office. "I need to talk to you and Graham."

Piper sighs and walks back to the counter. "What's up?"

"We're entering the Christmas parade this year, that's what's up."

I frown. "But you're always saying you don't have enough time to build a float that people are going to gawk at for ten minutes and then never see again."

"I don't," Aunt Bee says. "But that's what having employees is for, and now that I have two really good ones, I'm putting the brunt of the work on your very young and capable shoulders."

I sputter. "But the parade's on Christmas Eve—that's eight days from now. We couldn't possibly build an entire float in that amount of time."

"Sure you can. Bob's Grocers can knock one out in two days."

"They have six people on staff, not to mention his entire family helps out."

"Good thing you have six days, then, huh?"

Piper bites her lip. "I hate to say this, Aunt Bee, since I just started working here and I really love my job and all, but I have cheerleading practice, and winter break doesn't start until Wednesday, and—"

Aunt Bee puts her hands on her hips. "There's a Christmas bonus of one hundred bucks in it for each of you, plus overtime pay. I've already set up a space for you to work in my ex-husband's barn from seven to nine in the evenings on weekdays and all day tomorrow and next Sunday."

"But the store doesn't close on Sundays," I say.

"And?"

"And … can you handle the Sunday crowd all by yourself?"

"Well, let's see. I've owned this bookstore for almost forty years now, and before that I worked as a salesgirl in countless stores, so yes, Graham, I think I can handle two Sundays all by my lonesome. So, if you've finished questioning your boss, I expect the two of you to set up a time to meet tonight to discuss your ideas so you can get started on it right away. I'll give Graham the details on our budget and the address of the barn."

"Yes, ma'am," Piper says, looking at me from the corner of her eye.

I force a smile. "Sure. No problem."

Aunt Bee rolls her eyes. "You'd think I asked you both to walk across a bed of hot coals. Kids these days."

She saunters off, and I turn to Piper.

"You free tonight?"

"I was supposed to go to the movies with Jordan, but I can cancel."

Thank God. I don't even know why I hate Jordan so much or why the thought of them being kept apart gives me so much pleasure (not to mention it's really hypocritical of me considering I almost bit off Piper's head for pointing out Sarah's faults), but I can't help it. The guy just rubs me the wrong way.

"Yeah, okay," I say. "Let's grab that ice cream we talked about last week, and we'll figure out what we need and what it'll cost."

"All right. Text me when you get out of here."

"See you."

Business picks up after three o'clock, when the toy drive ends and the booths start dismantling. Mom stops by the store to do some Christmas shopping in the children's section for my younger cousins and tells me they've set a new record for donations to the children's hospital this year.

Sarah texts me not long after.

WE WON!!! We're heading out to get some celebration pizza (not that I can eat any). What do you want to do tonight?

I text back, letting her know about Piper and the parade float, but she doesn't respond and I can't help but wonder, Was Piper right? And even if she was, should I care? I mean, I haven't exactly been the poster child for chill when it comes to Sarah. Even now, I cringe when I think about how I must have sounded that night to her in the gazebo, before I made the wish that changed everything.

So what if Sarah has a jealous side? I was jealous of Jeremy for two years.

I shouldn't let it bother me, but it does. And what bothers me even more is the fact that I don't think I would have thought twice about it had Piper not said anything, which leads to an even more troubling thought:

Since when did I start caring so much about what Piper Hudson thinks?

7

***

At half past seven, I nudge my way through the swinging door into Nora's Old-Fashioned Ice Cream Parlor, push my hair—sopping wet from the sudden downpour—off my forehead, and order a hot chocolate with extra marshmallows. I spot Piper sitting at a table by the gigantic front window overlooking the square. The multicolored Christmas lights wrapped around the trees outside create a wall of color behind her, softened and haloed by the rain. She's reading that same book again, her umbrella hooked to the side of her chair, a small puddle underneath. She hasn't bought anything—probably because she's shivering too badly to even think about ice cream—so I ask for another hot chocolate and wind my way through the crowd to her table.

The chair scrapes as I pull it out and sit down across from her. "What's up with you and that book?"

She looks up. There's a slightly dazed expression on her face, as if she forgot where she was for a moment, and her bottom lip is red and swollen with teeth marks. "What do you mean?"

"You're reading it like you've never read it before," I say, handing her the hot chocolate. A froth of whipped cream slips over the side of the rim. "Completely oblivious to the world around you."

She puts the book and that little pencil in her purse, then swipes her finger over the whipped cream and licks it off, completely unaware that half the guys in the room just dropped their ice creams on themselves. She pulls one leg up on the chair and blows on the steam rising from her cup. "Is it a crime to like a book that much?"

"Not at all. It just seems rare these days."

Her mouth tugs up into a half smile. "Well, I guess I'm a little old-fashioned."

"And what's up with the note-taking? You'd think you wouldn't have anything new to write if you've read it so many times."

She takes a sip and makes a *hmm* sound in the back of her throat before setting the cup back down. "I went to this lecture once about interacting with the books you read. The professor said that writing notes in the margins is one of the best ways to retain the information, and I like seeing how my opinions change each time I read it."

I shake my head. "I've never met anyone so interested in learning anything that's not going to be on a test."

"I know," she says. "But life's a sort of test on it its own, right? Who knows when something I picked up from *Little Women* will come in handy?"

I blink.

She winces. "Sorry. I sound like a total nerd, right?"

"That's not a bad thing. I was actually just thinking how smart you sound." I lean back in my seat. "Way too smart for Christmas High, anyway. You should be in some fancy college prep school."

"I used to be. Before the divorce. That's where I heard the lecture."

I swear under my breath. "I'm sorry."

"Don't be. A lot's changed, but I can handle it." She swallows. "We should get down to business so we can both go home, don't you think?"

I cock my head toward the window as the rain picks up. "I don't think we'll be going anywhere for a while. It sounds like someone's pelting rocks at the roof."

"Well, it is hailing."

"Is it?" I glance out the window, where little balls of ice the size of marbles are ricocheting off the sidewalk. "Yep. That would explain it. I guess you're stuck with me."

She rolls her eyes. "Lucky me."

"Yeah, I deserve that. I was kind of a jerk earlier."

"No, you weren't," she says, pausing to take another sip of her hot chocolate. "I was being nosy. Truce?"

She sticks out her hand.

"Yeah," I say, taking it, my palm sliding across hers. "Truce."

She quickly tugs her hand away, pulling out a notebook and turning to a page covered in small sketches of floats and books and Christmas trees. "I've already started jotting down some ideas. I hope you don't mind."

My eyes widen. "You have experience with this whole float thing?"

"Um, hello? Cheerleader," she says, pointing to herself.

"Oh right," I say, scooting my chair closer. "So, what do we need?"

"Well, I was thinking we should come up with a theme, and with it being a bookstore and all, I thought we could create some of our favorite fictional characters surrounded by mountains and mountains of books, maybe piled on top of each other into Christmas tree shapes, like the one you made in the front window? We'll need some plywood, a bunch of chicken wire, and pretty much every scrap of papier-mâché from here to San Francisco, but I think we can pull it off."

"I'm game if you are."

We work for over an hour, sketching out different concepts and adding a children's books section in the front to showcase the importance of teaching children to love reading from an early age. The hail stops, but the rain comes down in sheets again as we sip our hot chocolates and watch it cascade off the red-and-white striped awning.

"Temperature's supposed to drop tonight," the busgirl says as she grabs our empty mugs from the table. "It'll be freezing rain in another hour and snow by midnight. Two to four inches. Maybe we'll get a white Christmas this year after all." She holds out the mugs. "Can I offer anyone a refill?"

Piper checks her watch. "Actually, I should get going. I told Queenie I'd be home ten minutes ago."

"None for me, thanks," I tell the girl.

She smiles and walks off.

I glance at the window and frown. "You don't have a car, do you?"

"No," Piper says, sweeping her notebook and cell into her purse. "You?"

"I'm saving up for one. I use my Dad's for my paper route, but it's not like a car is a real necessity in this town. Everything's a ten-minute walk from everything else. But a ten-minute walk in this weather's no joke."

Piper's brow arches. "Are you really worried about me, or are you just angling for an invitation to walk under my umbrella?"

"Both," I say, grinning. "Seriously though. Let me call my house and see if anyone can pick us up."

"That's really not necessary—"

"It's not a big deal."

I dial the house, but when it cuts over to the machine, I remember Dad's got his weekly bowling league tonight and Mom's got her monthly book club. Mom will be gone at least another hour—more if there are margaritas—and Dad doesn't pick up his cell when I call.

"No luck?" Piper asks as I hang up.

I shake my head.

"Well, thanks for trying."

"Wait. Where does your grandma live?"

"Cherry Street."

"Okay," I say. "Seems to me we've got two options. I can either walk you all the way over to Cherry Street in this"—I gesture through the window at the wall of water spewing off the awning, through which the individual tree lights have turned into sheets of stretched-out color, making the rain-soaked window look like a backlit water feature—"or we can head over to the bowling alley down the street and hitch a ride from my dad."

Her brow furrows. "Are you sure he won't mind?"

"Why would he mind?"

"I don't want to bother him if he's busy—"

"Trust me. He won't care. In fact, he'll be more pissed if I walk home in this without an umbrella and flood the entryway. And then Mom will be pissed because I'll get a cold, and you'll be saving me a lecture and a gallon of disgusting cold medicine if you just let me walk you to the bowling alley."

She shakes her head and laughs. "When you put it that way, how can a girl refuse?"

She bundles herself into her jacket, loops her scarf around her neck, and slings her purse across her body. I open the front door for her. The rain—which feels more like ice pellets strafing my skin—spews in as Piper holds out her umbrella in front of her, struggling with the mechanism until it finally catches, and we step through the door.

There's no one else outside in this weather, not even cars splashing by. The town is eerily silent aside from the raindrops battering the umbrella and the relentless howling of the wind, scooping up the rain and spitting it sideways. Piper compensates by holding the umbrella at an angle, but then the water sluicing down the awnings drenches us, so she gives up and holds it straight. The Christmas lights wrapped around the lampposts to either side of us blur, and across the street, the haze of the multicolored bulbs on the pines twinkle like splotches of paint against a black canvas. Over the square's speakers comes the garbled voice of Bing Crosby, telling us to have a merry little Christmas.

Piper's arm bumps mine as we shuffle awkwardly underneath the umbrella, and the fabric of our jacket sleeves swish against each other. I'm overly aware of Piper, the closeness of her, the scent of her hair as the wind whips it onto my shoulder. A gust rocks her back and her free hand grips my forearm as she steadies herself, and I wonder if she's as aware of me as I am of her. If she's feeling the same electric spark shooting up her arm and down her spine whenever we touch.

I clear my throat and shout, "It's that brick building over there!"

"What?" She turns her head toward me as I look at her, and her nose brushes my chin. She laughs. "Sorry!"

I try to laugh too—*Think of Sarah, think of Sarah, think of Sarah*—but my laugh sounds more like the terrified cries of a person with the hiccups being strangled. I point out the redbrick building with the neon bowling pin that reads, *Alley Cat Lane, Est. 1964*, and she nods.

We practically fall through the front door into the lobby, water dripping from our shoes, forming puddles on the black-and-white checkered tile. Piper tries to wrap up her umbrella, but that only squeezes more water onto the floor. The owner narrows his eyes at us from behind the counter. Piper gives him a crooked smile and waves.

It's a small bowling alley, just five lanes, and I spot Dad and his bowling league at lane one, sharing an extra-large pizza and a pitcher of beer.

"Hey, kid," Dad says, standing up and wiping his hands on a napkin. "Decide to take a shower in your clothes?"

"Kind of."

"And who's this lovely lady?"

Piper shakes Dad's hand politely, even though his fingers are still coated in pizza grease. "Piper Hudson. I work with Graham at the bookstore."

"Any relation to Mary Lou Hudson?"

Piper brightens, as if Dad just mentioned her favorite thing in the entire world. "That's my grandma."

"That's right," Dad says. "Mary Lou told me her grand-daughter was coming to stay with her a couple months ago. Welcome to Christmas."

"Thank you, Mr. Wallace."

"So." Dad sinks back into his seat. "What brings you two by the bowling alley? Everything okay?"

"It's pouring," I tell him. "We were a couple doors down at Nora's, getting some work done for Aunt Bee, and I told Piper you'd give us a ride home so she wouldn't have to walk all the way to Cherry Street in this mess."

"If," Piper says quickly, "it isn't a problem."

"Of course it's not a problem. But the boys and I are in the middle of a best-two-out-of-three game with one more to go, so it'll be a while yet."

"That's okay," Piper says. "I'll just give my grandma a call and let her know what's going on."

Piper pulls out her phone and walks away from Dad's

bowling league buddies, who are now singing along with the jukebox to "Come On, Eileen" at the top of their lungs.

Dad elbows me and fishes his wallet out of his pocket. "Why don't you two play a game on me?"

"You don't have to do that—"

"Son, you know how long it takes these guys to finish a game when they've got a couple beers in them. Don't make that poor girl wait around in this disgusting hole-in-the-wall—and I mean that with the utmost respect, Danny," he says as the owner passes by, shooting Dad a dirty look, "—when she can have some fun."

"Yeah," I say, taking a twenty from him. "Okay. Thanks."

I take the cash up to the counter and buy a game. Danny tucks an unlit cigarette behind his long hair and says, his voice gruff as sandpaper, "Lane five. Shoe size?"

"Eleven," I say, watching Piper pace in front of the doors, a finger in her ear to drown out the music as she speaks into her phone.

She laughs at something her grandma says, then mouths, "Okay, bye," and hangs up.

"What's your shoe size?" I ask as she walks over.

"Seven," she says. "Are we playing?"

"You don't have to. If you just like sitting around in bowling shoes, that's fine too. I won't judge."

"I'm not the best player."

"Have you checked out the loud, drunk, middle-aged men on lane one? Because they're horrific."

She glances at them, and I'm mortified to see Dad with his shirt rolled up, rubbing his belly for good luck. He gets into position, glides forward, and lets the ball fly—

Straight into the gutter.

"Oh yeah," I say. "You're in good company."

"Har har."

Danny hands over her shoes, shiny with disinfectant, and

she hooks her fingers into the heels. "I don't have to rub my stomach before I throw, do I?"

I get a sudden picture of Piper rolling up her shirt and quickly shove it away, clearing my throat. "Not unless you thought my dad looked cool doing it. In which case, I think your lack of bowling talent is the least of your worries."

I lead the way to lane five. We slip into our shoes and pick our balls from the rack.

"You want to go first?" I ask.

"Okay," she says, "but don't laugh. I've only done this once before."

My mouth drops. "In your entire life?"

"Um. Yeah?"

"How is that possible?"

She looks down at the ball in her hands and shrugs. "My parents were always busy."

"Well, how about we see what you've got, and then I can help if you need it."

"Okay . . ."

She steps up to the line and looks at the floor.

"What do these arrows mean?" she asks.

"Wow, you really are a noob."

She glares at me.

I laugh and hold up my hands. "They're to help you aim."

"Oh. Is there a specific one I should focus on?"

"Everyone has a different style, especially when you get comfortable and start putting some spin on the ball—" I break off at her confused look. "I would just stick to the middle one for now."

She nods, backs up two paces, swings her arm back, and moves forward, releasing the ball. It doesn't go two feet before slamming into the gutter and bouncing into the next lane.

"Sorry!" she yells at the guys in lane four. They all turn to her with wide eyes, but I'm not sure if they're impressed with her gusto, terrified by her proximity to them, or struck dumb by how cute she looks standing there, mortified, her hands thrown up, a pink flush to her cheeks.

"Uh, no biggie," one of them says, retrieving her ball from their return. I take it from him and join Piper in front of the lane.

She bites her lip. "That was bad, wasn't it?"

"Nah."

She gives me a look.

"Yeah, it was pretty bad," I say. "But we can work on it."

I stand behind her, completely ignoring the warmth of her body against mine, not even noticing that rich, jasmine scent of her perfume that makes my head spin in the best possible way. I place my hand over hers—her knuckles push against my palm—and guide her through the motions.

"You want to keep your wrist straight," I tell her, "and let your thumb guide the ball."

She glances back at me over her shoulder, her breath warm against my neck. "I think I've got it now."

I swallow and take a step back. "Yeah, okay. Try it out."

She pulls the ball up in front of her and takes her first step, swinging the ball back. On her second step, she starts the down-swing, then bends a little in the knee like I taught her and lets it fly. She only knocks down four pins, but she manages to stay away from the gutter.

She jumps up. "I did it!"

"That was fantastic!"

She runs forward like she's going to hug me, and for a split second I open my arms, but then we both stop, and she puts her hands in her back pockets instead.

"Uh, it's your turn now, right?" she asks.

"Right. I mean—" I shake my head. "No. You get one more throw, since you technically didn't throw your first ball in our lane."

"Oh, yeah. Okay."

Her second ball takes the same trajectory as the first, only taking down one more pin. She gets better as the game progresses, picking up a spare in the sixth frame. I'm pretty rusty, and almost every strike I go for ends up with a seven-ten split, a shot I've never even gotten close to making before, but Piper seems impressed by my efforts anyway.

"I'm starving," she says as I walk back to my seat in front of the monitor. "You want some fries or something?"

My stomach rumbles. "Yeah, sure."

I stand up, but she waves me back down.

"I'll get it," she says. "You bought the game."

"Actually, my dad did," I say, feeling a little guilty, even though I know that's ridiculous. I shouldn't feel guilty for not paying for the game. It's not like this is a date or something.

Still.

"I'll get the fries," I say.

"Okay, how about this. You get the fries, I get the drinks?"

"Deal."

Once we're settled back at the table behind our lane with our fries and Cokes, Piper leans back in her chair and says, "Tell me something about yourself, Graham."

"Like what?" I ask, ripping open packets of ketchup and squeezing them into the corner of the paper container.

She pulls one leg up onto her chair and swirls a fry through the ketchup. "What kind of movies do you like?"

I pause, thinking. "Comedies and action, mostly."

"Shocker."

"That sounds like sarcasm, Hudson."

"That's because it is, Wallace."

"Okay, let me guess. Your favorite movies are romantic comedies, but you like to throw in *The Notebook* or some equally sad movie whenever you want to feel terrible for the rest of the night."

"I like them all right," she says, "but my absolute favorite movies, the ones I always go back to, are old musicals."

My brow arches. "Seriously? Like Gene Kelly and Fred Astaire?"

"And Howard Keel and Danny Kaye and Vera-Ellen."

"I don't know who any of those people are."

She laughs. "Okay, well, what's your favorite movie, then, assuming you can narrow it down from your eclectic taste of comedies and action? Wait, wait. Let me guess. *Die Hard*?"

"*Die Hard* is a fine film, but no."

"*Lethal Weapon?*"

"Which one?"

"The first one?"

"Also a fine film, but not my favorite."

She narrows her eyes. "The second? Third? *Fourth?*"

"Do you want the answer, or do you want to keep guessing?"

"Okay, fine," she says, swirling another fry. "What is it?"

"*The Shawshank Redemption.*"

She pauses.

Then: "I was getting to that one."

"You were not."

"I totally was!"

We both laugh and reach for a fry, our hands brushing as we grab the same one. I let go and lean back in my chair. "It's all yours."

She shakes her head, wiping her hands on a napkin. "You take it. I'm supposed to be bowling anyway."

She jumps up and heads over to the ball return, picking up her ball and getting into position. My phone buzzes in my pocket. A text from Sarah.

Hey, cutie. Whatcha doin?

I hesitate, then write back: Hanging out with my dad's bowling league. Heading home soon. You?

It's not a lie exactly, but that doesn't make me feel any less guilty. Still, it just seems like a bad idea to tell her Piper's here with me after what happened this afternoon.

She replies: Thinking about you.

And now I feel like the douchiest boyfriend ever. Before I can think what to say next, my phone buzzes again.

Are we hanging out tomorrow? Or are you going to be too busy building that float?

There's a sharp crack as a ball hits some pins, and then Piper's jumping up and down, shouting, "Graham! I got a strike!"

I glance up at her, distracted. "That's nice."

She stops jumping.

I type back: How about dinner tomorrow? We'll get burgers or something.

Sarah texts back: Sounds great. Love you!

Piper plops into her chair across from me, sweeping her hair to the side. "You're up, Shawshank."

My heart stops at the sight of her, and suddenly my body feels like it's in free fall, like that feeling you get when you jump off a cliff in a dream and you jerk awake. Heart beating fast, eyes scanning the darkness, brain wondering where the heck you are when just two seconds ago you were standing on top of a cliff.

What am I doing? I'm finally dating the girl of my dreams—and apparently I've impressed her enough over the past two years to make her fall in love with me even though I don't remember any of it—and I've been . . . oh God.

I've been flirting with another girl all night.

It was in no way a conscious decision. It just sort of happened.

Calm down, Graham, I tell myself. You didn't do anything

wrong. It's not like you and Piper kissed or anything.

But then, as quickly as it came, my attraction to Piper fades, and I realize I was just shaken up earlier by the whole tree-decorating thing with Sarah's family, and I forgot, for just a second, how lucky I am. I mean, my wish was granted for a reason, right? Sarah and I are supposed to be together. I'm just learning new things about her, and now that I've experienced her competitiveness firsthand, I'll know how to handle it next time.

Piper's just a friend. Not even that, really. We're coworkers. We wouldn't even be here, hanging out in a bowling alley and sharing fries, if Aunt Bee hadn't asked us to work on that float. So, whatever's going on with my brain that's making me want to sniff her perfume every five seconds (which really has nothing to do with liking how *she* smells but how the perfume smells anyway) and making my body tense up, extra alert, whenever we touch, it needs to stop. Now.

Love you too, I text back, and it feels like more than just a declaration. It feels like a reminder.

I love Sarah Clarke.

I shove my phone back into my pocket and glance over at lane one. "Looks like Dad's league's wrapping up. We should probably hurry through these last frames."

"Oh. Okay." Piper crosses her arms. "No problem."

"Hey," I say. "We're friends, right?"

"Yeah. Of course."

"Okay, good. I just, you know, wanted to make sure."

She nods, and I hurry over to the ball return, not even giving a second thought to the fact that the guys in the lane next to ours—guys, I might add, who are hovering around thirty and most of whom have wedding bands—are checking out Piper. Or so I think, until my foot slips and—

Great. Gutter ball.

✳✳✳

I pull up to Mrs. Hudson's house on Cherry Street, a little white bungalow with a wide porch and turquoise shutters. There aren't a lot of decorations out, just a silver wreath on the front door and white twinkle lights around the porch columns. The rain has switched to a light snow, just barely sticking to the grass, and Piper keeps her now mostly dry umbrella closed as she opens the door and jumps out. "Thanks for the ride, Mr. Wallace."

"Anytime, Piper," Dad says from the passenger seat. He drank even more than usual with his buddies as soon as he realized I'd be his designated driver. "Does your grandma need help putting up her lights? I seem to remember her having a lot more than just those flimsy little twinkle ones."

"She does, she just can't put them up like she used to. I did the ones on the porch."

He hiccups. "Not to worry. I'll send Graham over sometime this week, and he'll put up the rest for her."

Piper hesitates, her eyes sliding to mine. "You don't have to—"

"It's okay," I say. "I don't mind."

"Okay. Well. Thanks."

She closes the door and heads for the porch.

Dad clears his throat.

"Yes?" I ask.

"Aren't you going to walk her to the door?"

"This wasn't a date, Dad."

"Jumpy tonight, aren't you?"

"I already have a girlfriend, if you haven't forgotten."

"Well, date or not, I taught my son better than to let a girl walk up to her front door all by her lonesome."

"Dad—"

"Get out of the car, Graham."

I sigh. "Yes, sir."

I jump out and slam the door shut. Piper stops searching through her purse and looks back at me from the porch.

"What's up?" she asks.

"Nothing." I come to a stop in front of her.

"Seriously, what are you doing?"

"I'm supposed to walk you to your door."

"Your dad knows this wasn't a date, right?"

"That's what I told him. But he's old-fashioned, and I guess that isn't an entirely terrible way to be."

Her lips quirk into that half smile she always seems to get around me. "Not at all." She pulls her key out and slips it into the lock. "Well, I had fun tonight. Thanks for the ride."

"No problem."

"You have my number, right? So we can get together tomorrow?"

"Yeah, and Aunt Bee gave me the address of that barn. I figured I'd pick you up and we'd head over together. Around ten work for you?"

"Better make it nine," she says. "We have to stock up on supplies beforehand, and I don't want to be there all day."

"Hot date with Jason tomorrow night?"

"*Jordan.* And no, actually. I'm going dress shopping with Queenie."

"For the dance?"

She nods. "I ran into Jeremy when I left the bookstore, and he asked me."

"And Josh won't mind?"

"Jordan, and I don't see why he would. We've only gone on a couple dates, and—why are you looking at me like that?"

For the love of God, Graham, whatever you do, don't say what you're actually thinking.

"I just—I mean—" I take a deep breath. "I figured you had guys lining up all over town to take you, being a cheerleader and all, but it's one thing to *think* it and another thing to see it. Not that I care or anything," I say quickly. "You can date whoever you want—"

"Thanks for the permission."

I wince. "That's not what I meant. I just"—*Wrap it up, Einstein*—"I'm glad you're going to the dance."

She rolls her eyes. "Please. Jeremy only asked me because you talked him into it."

"No, I didn't—"

"Hey, I'm not complaining. I didn't want to be the only person in town without a date. How embarrassing would that have been?"

"Yeah," I say, scratching the back of my neck. "Pretty pathetic."

She grins. "Okay, well. Good night."

"Night."

She twists the knob and steps inside, closing the door behind her.

I walk back to the car, hands in my pockets. I don't realize I'm still smiling until I slide behind the wheel and Dad says, "You look pretty happy for someone who wasn't on a date."

"How about we play the silent game for the rest of the night?"

Dad laughs. "That stopped working on you when you were five. It's not going to work on me at forty-six."

I sigh as I turn back onto Main Street. "A kid can dream."

8

✳✳✳

*D*ad's catching up on some work at the office after church the next morning, so I ask Mom if I can use her car. The barn's address is only four blocks southeast of Main Street, just outside of town, where the old Victorian and craftsman houses give way to farmland as far as the eye can see. An easy-enough walk if you have nothing to take with you that won't fit inside a backpack, but we'll need the car today to transport our supplies. Mom agrees, but she has to run to the grocery store first, so I'm fifteen minutes late pulling into Piper's driveway, tires crunching the inch of snow that managed to stick to the asphalt after last night's rain.

"Sorry I'm late," I say as Piper opens her front door.

"No biggie," she says, then calls over her shoulder, "I'll be back later, Queenie."

"Wait a second," her grandma answers, followed by the sound of a recliner footrest closing. "I want to thank Graham for putting up my decorations."

"Hi, Mrs. Hudson," I say as she comes to the door carrying

a plate of cookies.

"He's not putting the decorations up today, Queenie—"

"I *know* that," Mrs. Hudson says. "My knees may be shot, but my hearing works just fine. I just need to get these cookies out of the house before I eat them all. Here you go, Graham."

I take the plate. "Thanks, Mrs. Hudson."

"Now you two be good," she says, wagging her finger at me. "And don't even think about getting fresh with my granddaughter, sonny."

The plate fumbles in my hand and several cookies slide off. "Uh—"

"We're not dating, Queenie," Piper says.

"He's not the one who's been taking you to the coffee shop?"

"No."

Mrs. Hudson narrows her eyes. "Oh, so he's the one you're going to the dance with?"

Piper shakes her head. "Graham's dating Sarah Clarke, remember?"

Mrs. Hudson's eyes slide to mine. She shakes her head slowly, and for a moment, I think, *She knows.* But then her face clears and she says, "Oh yes, right. Of course. How could I forget? I guess I really am getting old."

Piper rolls her eyes and grabs my hand. She leads me off the porch and onto the walkway, her boots trampling over the outline of my footsteps in the snow. "Come on, Graham. See you later, Queenie."

"Don't do anything I wouldn't do," she calls after us with a little, cackling sort of laugh. She looks down at the broken cookies on the porch, then waves her hand and mutters, "Let the birds have them."

"Sorry about that," Piper says, sliding into the passenger seat as Queenie disappears back inside her house. "In her mind, it doesn't mean a thing that you've been dating

Sarah for two years. You know, 'boys will be boys' and all that sexist nonsense."

"Well, I promise to give you fair warning if I feel like getting fresh," I joke, placing the plate out of harm's way in the back seat.

We both chuckle but it's forced, and suddenly I'm thinking about getting "fresh" with Piper Hudson, and I know she's thinking about it too.

"Music?" I pop on the radio before she can answer.

"Oh, I love this song!" She turns up the radio and starts singing, "On the first day of Christmas, my true love sent to me..."

"A partridge in a pear tree," I join in using a fake deep baritone.

Piper throws back her head and laughs, and by the time we pull into the hardware store, we're trying to outdo each other on how fast we can sing the lyrics, until it's all just one long string of unintelligible sounds.

I turn off the car, my eyes watering. "I don't even know why we're laughing so hard."

"Me neither," Piper says, clutching her stomach.

"Sarah hates that song."

"Oh?"

"Yeah, she thinks it's annoying."

Piper's quiet for a moment. Then she smiles. "Well, it kind of is."

"Totally," I say, grinning back. "Come on. Let's get some chicken wire before they're sold out."

"Maybe we should just buy all of it for ourselves," Piper says. "Then we'll definitely have the best float in the parade."

"Ah, now you're getting into the Christmas spirit."

We don't buy all of the chicken wire, but there's enough to take up the entire trunk, so we have to pile our crepe paper, superglue, and the rest of our tools in the back seat.

"I hope we have enough," Piper says as we climb into the car, and I think she's kidding until I catch her biting her bottom lip.

"You'd be terrible at poker," I tell her, twisting the key into the ignition and pulling out of our parking space.

"What makes you say that?"

"You always bite your lip when you're worried."

"I do not!"

"Do too. You also do it when you're really into what you're reading."

"Well then, if we were playing poker, how would you know if I was worried about my cards or just 'really into' them?"

"Your cheeks."

"Excuse me?"

I clear my throat. "They, uh, turn pink when you're excited. Like when a new book comes out from one of your favorite authors, followed immediately by the lip biting because now the presence of a new book has totally messed up your system of which book to buy next."

She doesn't respond.

I glance over at her. "Am I right?"

"You've been watching me a lot, haven't you?"

Crap. Have I? Does it take a lot of watching to notice those kinds of things about a person? And if it does, what does it say about me that those are things I've noticed? Should I be noticing those things about a girl who's not my girlfriend?

"Not a lot," I say quickly. "I mean, when you work long hours with someone, you can't really help but notice a couple things. Here and there. Right?"

"You always remembered which books I'd looked through the week before when I'd come to the bookstore."

"I did?"

"And sometimes you'd read them before me, just to let

me know if they were worth getting or not."

I frown. Sure, I did that in the alternate universe, when I wasn't dating Sarah, but it wasn't because I *liked* Piper or anything. She just made me ... curious. The way she'd waffle between which book she wanted to buy, some days for over an hour. I'd never seen a customer so torn. Most people came into the store knowing exactly what they wanted or else had the money to buy several books that struck their fancy, but Piper was always very concerned about spending money on only one book a week. I'd wanted to ask her if that was all she got in allowance or something, but it had seemed rude at the time.

I never thought I would have still paid so much attention to Piper in a universe where I'd been dating Sarah for two years. Why would I? I mean, shouldn't I have been obsessed with Sarah this whole time? Texting her during work instead of noticing the new girl in town, or planning my next date with her, or ... something?

I clear my throat and try for a light, carefree tone. "Sorry. Didn't realize I was such a creeper."

"It wasn't creepy," she says. "It was nice."

"Oh."

The rest of the drive is silent aside from the Christmas music streaming from our town's "most listened-to radio station", WCHR. Piper taps her fingers on the armrest to the beat, and I tap mine on the steering wheel. We don't look at each other, but then it becomes obvious that we're not looking at each other, so I glance at her, and she glances at me, and I blurt out, "First real snow of the season."

She turns her head to look at the snow dusting the grass. "Yep."

I lean forward, glancing up at the thick gray clouds through the windshield. "Looks like we might get more later."

Her lips twitch. "Yep."

"And that's it for me on the small-talk portion of our morning." I lean back in my seat, flicking on my turn signal as I pull onto a country road lined with bare birch trees. "Your turn."

"My turn for what?"

"To think of something asinine to say."

"That's all right. You're doing a good enough job for the both of us."

"Har har."

She giggles.

The road takes a sharp curve, and I spot the red barn behind a square two-story house with a wraparound porch. It's situated on a Christmas tree farm, with fir trees in varying stages of growth darkening the landscape on either side of the road. The Christmas tree lot sits across the street from the house, outlined in a white picket fence. The sign outside it reads *OPEN DAILY 10–6*, and there are already cars parked in the grass waiting for it to open, clouds of exhaust swirling from their tailpipes.

"There it is," I say, nodding my head toward the barn.

"Wow," Piper says, sitting up straighter. "It's gorgeous. Have you been here before?"

I shake my head. "Mom prefers fake trees. Aunt Bee talks about it sometimes though. She's on pretty good terms with her ex-husband. They still own the business fifty-fifty. He owns half the bookstore too."

"Wow. Why did they get a divorce?"

"Not sure. People around town like to talk, so I've heard rumors, but if you live in this town long enough, you learn not to trust everything you hear."

Piper nods as I pull into the drive. An older man wearing a green flannel shirt and a plaid cap with ear flaps strides through the front door of the house, locking up behind him.

"You Beatrice's kids?" he asks as he starts down the porch

steps.

"Yes, sir, Mr. Campbell," I say, running up to shake his hand. "I'm Graham Wallace, and this is Piper Hudson."

"It's a pleasure to meet you," Piper says.

He nods. "Well, barn's all yours, and there's some tools you can use if need be. Beatrice's already got the flatbed trailer set up in there, so all you got to do is build the dang thing." He smiles, deepening the wrinkles around his mouth and eyes. "Well, holler if you need me. I'll be across the street."

We thank him and unload the car. Once everything's inside the barn—which has some empty stalls that used to hold horses but are now used for storage—and Piper has double-checked that everything's accounted for, I cross my arms and say, "Now what?"

She stuffs her list into her purse and places it on the floor next to a space heater that either Mr. Campbell or Aunt Bee had the good sense to turn on before we arrived.

"Now," she says, "we build the frame."

✳✳✳

After a lot of false starts and muttered cursing, we finally figure out the general shape we want the chicken wire to take around the flatbed. Another few hours go by and we've gotten half the skirt covered in red-and-green crepe paper and Piper has started cutting out letters to spell *Merry Christmas from Aunt Bee's Bookstore* on either side of the float.

My stomach grumbles. I check my phone.

Two o'clock.

"Whoa. No wonder I'm so hungry."

Piper looks up from the workstation she's made out of a piece of plywood on top of two cobwebbed sawhorses. "Huh?"

I show her the time. "You want to grab something to eat?"

"Sure," she says, setting down her scissors. She's spotlighted by the light bulb hanging over her, creating a shimmering, golden halo that bounces off her blonde hair and white cable-knit sweater. "What were you thinking?"

"There's a pizza place just outside of town, about half a mile from here. It's not mind-blowing pizza or anything, but it's cheap and tastes all right. Not that I don't mind spending a little more if you, uh, wanted something better—"

Her eyes lock on mine, and she gives me that familiar half smile, the one that makes me think she can see right through me.

The one that makes me want to ask her what she sees.

"Cheap's fine. I'm not exactly made of cash either. And I still owe you gas money for bringing me out here."

"Oh, no, that's not necessary—"

"Speaking of," she says, hitching her purse onto her shoulder so that the strap cuts diagonally across her chest, "how about we walk to this pizza place?"

My brow arches. "I'm not *that* much of a cheapskate."

She laughs. "That's not what I meant. It's just, if it's only half a mile, I thought it might be nice to walk. Maybe cut through the trees. I've never been to a Christmas tree farm before."

"Your parents like fake trees too?"

"Mom likes the all-white kind, and she likes all of her Christmas ornaments and wrapping paper color-coordinated in tiffany blue and silver. It looks nice, but Dad hates it because it costs a lot of money to make sure everything matches, and I hate it because there's nothing personal about it. No 'Baby's First Christmas' ornaments or ornaments from places we've visited together as a family. It just . . . I don't know . . . never felt very festive. It was like we only had a tree because that's what was expected, and if we were going to go to the trouble of having a tree, it might as well look like it came from a catalog . . ." She trails off, staring at her hands as she picks at the barn dust beneath her fingernails.

I clear my throat. "Yeah. Let's walk."

"Really?"

I nod.

Her eyes brighten. "Okay."

I shrug into my coat, and we set out from the barn, cutting across the yard onto a path lined by six-foot-tall fir trees. I can just barely see over the top of them to the road and the tree lot beyond. The thickness of the trees surrounding us blocks out the sounds of the rest of the world so that we hear nothing but the crunch of our boots on frosted snow and the creaking of tree branches in the wind and the swirling fog of our collective breaths.

I shove my hands into my pockets as the cold air bites my flesh. I make a mental note that it's officially glove weather—there's nothing sexy about frostbite.

The quiet stretches between us until it starts to get to that awkward stage, both of us fidgeting slightly, darting quick glances and crooked smiles. *Come on, Graham. You're an okay student. Surely you can think of* something *to say other than "looks like snow" again.*

"Are your parents going to visit for Christmas?" I ask.

She scoffs. "Not likely. Dad might, since Queenie is his mom, but we haven't really talked about it. This is my parents' busiest time of year anyway, even if they weren't in the middle of their own divorce. Everyone wants all their papers squared away with their lawyers before New Year's, and they don't typically realize it until halfway through December. So yeah, it's no biggie. I'm kind of used to it."

I don't know what to say to this. "I'm sorry" feels too general, and I can't exactly empathize with her, not in a town where everyone breathes Christmas 365 days a year. Not just because it's the name of our town or because it's "the most wonderful time of the year" but because it's a holiday centered around love and family, and this town—for all of its gossip and weird quirks—is like one big family, so no one who lives here is ever really alone on Christmas. Not to mention my parents (for all the crap I give Mom for her over-the-top Christmas enthusiasm and all the crap I give Dad for loving Mom too much to tell her to stop blaring her music so loud in the morning) have always been there for me, and for each other, so I really can't fathom the depth of the pain she's feeling.

So instead, I just say, "Oh. Well. That sucks."

A small, hiccup of laughter bursts out of her. "Yeah, it kind of does. But they're really not so bad. My whole family's just going through a tough time right now, so it's kind of easy to make them out to be these Scrooges who don't care about anything other than themselves when, really, they're not like that at all. In fact, we had one Christmas tradition my parents never broke, no matter how busy they were."

"Oh?"

The path narrows so that our shoulders bump every other step. Piper reaches out and runs her hand along the branches, breathing in the thick, earthy scent of pine needles.

"Every Christmas morning," she says, "we'd get up really early. An hour before sunrise. Mom would put on a pot of coffee and make me a cup of hot chocolate, and we'd drive to this pond thirty minutes from our house. It was always crowded during the day, with ice skaters and kids sledding down the hill next to it, but there was never anyone there at sunrise on Christmas morning. We'd skate and watch the sun come up, then drive home bundled up in blankets and unwrap our presents, and it didn't matter what we did for the rest of the day, if we stayed together as a family or if they had to go into the office, because we'd had the morning. Just the three of us."

A squirrel skitters across the path, an acorn in its mouth, leaving behind a trail of thumb-sized footprints.

"Anyway," she says, "enough about me. What does your family do on Christmas morning?"

"Nothing too unusual," I say. "Presents with coffee and cinnamon rolls for breakfast. Then my aunt and uncle usually drive in from Richmond with my grandparents, and Mom makes Christmas dinner. We went to their house one year instead, but there was a small oven fire no one likes to talk about and we wound up eating our Christmas dinner at a Chinese restaurant. Mom's been in charge of Christmas ever since."

"Sounds nice."

"Yeah," I say. "It is."

She looks down as we walk, her shoulders hunched. I don't know what to say to make it better. I don't think there really is anything to say when your parents are getting a divorce. But then I stop, rising up on my toes to scan the street.

Piper stops when she realizes I'm not walking next to her anymore. "What's up?"

"There's something I want to show you. It should be just through the trees here." I reach my hand toward her without thinking, and I know I should drop it, but it feels like the most natural thing in the world, so I let it linger in the air between us, my heart racing. "Come on."

She swallows, then threads her fingers through mine. "Okay."

It isn't far, about a five-minute walk from the road. I lead Piper through the trees and try not to think about the electricity shooting up my arm or how aware I am of her palm pressed against mine.

I clear my throat. "It's, uh, right through here," I say, pushing aside boughs of evergreen needles. Piper lets go of my hand and steps through the trees, gasping as she takes in the large, man-made irrigation pond surrounded by birch trees.

"Old Man Turlington owns this pond—that's his farmhouse back there—but he lets kids come and swim in it during the summer, and a bunch of us skate on it in the winter." The water lapping the edge is just beginning to show signs of freezing, with thin snowflake-shaped ice fragments rimming the grass. "It probably won't be frozen come Christmas, but by January, you'll be able to skate to your heart's content."

"It's perfect." Her voice wobbles, and I'm surprised to see tears in her eyes. "Thank you."

She gives me a rare full smile, and my heart skips a beat.

"Yeah. Well. We should probably find that pizza place before we get gangrene."

She takes a step back. "Yeah. Okay."

She seems lighter now as we walk back the way we came, and even though my hands are numb and my ears feel like they're about to fall off, our little detour was worth it, just to make her smile.

Still, guilt presses on my chest like a heavy blanket, and I wipe my hand on the side of my pants, trying to rid myself of the feeling of Piper's fingers interlocked with mine.

✳✳✳

I pick up Sarah at eight o'clock for our date after dropping off Piper at home. We made good progress on the float, but it'll be a miracle if we have it done by Christmas Eve. It helped that we barely spoke after getting pizza, both of us ignoring the whole hand-holding incident the best we could, putting all of our energy into the float instead. At one point my hand brushed hers as I reached for the stapler and a charge of electricity zapped our fingers.

"The air sure is dry in here," I said, like I was on freaking *Leave It to Beaver* or something.

Golly gee willikers, Piper, I sure am sorry I'm such a MORON.

But other than that, there was absolutely no hand-holding or accidental touching. Still, I'd had a hard time concentrating on my work. All I kept thinking about, circling my mind like a vulture over a fresh kill, was: *What the hell is wrong with me?* I'm not much of a hand-holder to begin with. Every time Sarah tries to hold my hand, my palm gets all sweaty and I can never find a position for my freakishly large fingers that doesn't feel like I'm choking the life out of her tiny hand. But with Piper, I didn't even think about what I was doing as I led her to Old Man Turlington's pond. My hand didn't get sweaty, and my fingers linked through hers as if they had been designed to do so, which was why I didn't even really think about the fact that I have a girlfriend and probably shouldn't be holding another girl's hand until it was too late.

There must be some secret to hand-holding. Some maneuver that just happened naturally with Piper because I wasn't overanalyzing what I was doing. This thought stays with me when I ring Sarah's doorbell, and when she opens the door, I tell myself, *Don't think, just do*, thrust my hand out, and snatch her fingers in mine.

"Ow!" She pulls her hand back. "What was that for?"

"Sorry, just trying something," I say, heat rising up my neck. "You ready?"

She rubs her knuckles. "Um, yeah."

She closes the door behind her, her flat furry boots shuffling across the wooden boards of her front porch. I walk next to her down the walkway, my arm brushing hers—

Smooth, be smooth—and gently clasp her hand.

Okay! Definitely not terrible. At least I don't feel like I'm crushing her delicate ballerina fingers in my giant catcher's mitt of a palm.

"Your mom let you borrow her car?" she asks.

"Well, she technically said I could drive it to take Piper out to Mr. Campbell's barn, but I told her we'd be working late, so I doubt she's made any plans."

"Oh."

"Besides, it's cold out and my lady deserves the finest chariot this side of Second Street, and since Mr. Bambino's Jaguar is unavailable, our 'ninety-eight Accord will have to do."

"You forgot Miss Lawrence's Miata."

"Oh yeah," I say, opening the passenger side door for her. "Remind me to ask what the two of them do for a living. I haven't decided on a major yet."

She laughs and rolls her eyes.

"I'm serious."

"I know you are," she says, sliding into her seat. "That's why it's so funny."

I close her door and hurry over to the driver's side.

"So," she asks as I turn the key in the ignition, "how did everything go today? Did you finish the float?"

"Ha! No. We're a long way from finishing it, but we made some good progress."

"So, you and Piper are going to be spending a lot more time together, then?" There's a forced lightness to her tone. It's pretty good actually—really Oscar-worthy—but I know her too well not to hear it.

"Are you ... upset about that?"

"No," she says. "No, no, no."

"That's a lot of *nos*."

"That's because I mean it. I'm glad you're spending so

much time together. She doesn't seem to have that many friends for someone so popular."

"Uh-huh."

"I mean, she's so pretty and all, and she seems nice enough when you first meet her, but . . ."

"But?"

"Well, she must be really bitchy or self-centered or something. I mean, how can you live here for four months and not have any friends, or even a boyfriend?"

I exhale. "Wow."

"What?"

I know I shouldn't say it—I should keep my mouth shut and accept that this jealous side is something I'll have to get used to—but I can't let her say things about Piper that aren't true.

"Well," I say, taking a deep breath, "that was kind of a 'really bitchy' thing to say."

I steel myself for the anger I know is coming as I pull into a parking spot outside the diner, but Sarah surprises me by sighing.

"I know," she says, "I'm sorry. I just miss you. I feel like we haven't been spending a lot of time together lately."

I frown. "You were over at my house every day last week."

"Yeah, but you seem—I don't know—different somehow."

Crap. Have I been doing something wrong? Have I been acting like the me I was in my previous life and not like the me I've been here?

Man, this is getting confusing.

"Different how?" I ask.

"Distant," she says. "Unsure of yourself. I know it's the holiday season and you have a lot on your plate, but I feel like you're drifting away from me, and Piper's really pretty and you're spending so much time together at the bookstore, and now you'll be spending even *more* time together while

I'm spending every spare minute at practice, and I just—"

I silence her with a kiss, pressing my hands to either side of her face. Her lips meld with mine, and in this, in the pressing of our lips together, in the smooth slide of our tongues, we fit perfectly. I pull away, our noses still touching, and say, "You're my dream girl, Sarah. I've been in love with you since before you even knew I existed. How can you think for one second any girl could compare to you?"

Her lips twitch. "You really mean that?"

"You know I do. It's always been you."

She takes a deep breath, resting her forehead against mine. "Sorry I've been such a paranoid, jealous girlfriend. I'll cut it out now, I swear."

"Okay," I say. "And as soon as the float is finished and the holiday rush is over at the store, I'm going to spend every waking second I can with you. I'll even sit in the waiting room at your ballet studio on my days off and read those girly magazines while you're practicing so I don't get bored."

"Oh yeah. Act like that's why you're reading them."

"What can I say? Those 'What Kind of a Girlfriend Are You?' quizzes just get me on a personal level."

"Don't forget the 'What's Your Patronus?' quizzes."

"Meerkat all the way, baby."

She laughs.

"Come on," I say, tucking a strand of hair behind her ear. "Let's get something to eat. I'm starving."

"Me too. This diet is killing me."

I dart out of the car and rush around to open the door for her. She thanks me with a peck on the cheek.

The walls of the retro 1950's diner are covered in old records and pictures of Elvis, Marilyn Monroe, James Dean, and other classic actors and rock stars. An aluminum Christmas tree is set up in the corner, decorated with shiny vintage ornaments. There's mistletoe hanging over every table and the Rat Pack is singing "Jingle Bells" on the jukebox, and the thought *Piper would like it here* pops into my head before I can stop it.

We slide into a red pleather booth and pull out our menus from behind the napkin dispenser. I scan the options but I already know what I want, and I quickly put it back.

"Getting your usual?" Sarah asks.

"You know it."

I briefly wonder if my "usual" in this alternate universe is the same as my "usual" from before, but I decide it doesn't really matter. Even though I've woken up every morning this past week wondering if this will be the day everything goes back to normal, there hasn't been a reason so far to think that this whole wish-upon-a-star thing isn't going to stick, so I should really stop thinking about myself as before-the-wish Graham and after-the-wish Graham and just start living. If I screw up and find out I really do have a different usual here, I'll just cover it by saying I felt like something different.

Bottom line: I need to stop freaking out that I'm going to do something wrong and just enjoy the ride.

The waiter comes over to take our orders. I get a double cheeseburger with everything on it, a large basket of fries, and a chocolate milkshake. The waiter turns to Sarah.

"I'll take a side salad, no dressing," she says.

The waiter writes down her order and walks away.

"You sick or something?"

She leans back in her seat. "What do you mean?"

"The Sarah I know would have ordered everything I did *plus* a basket of jalapeno poppers, and she would have downed it all just to make me feel like less of a man."

Ten seconds. That's how long it took for me to compare this alternate universe to my previous reality.

Great job, Graham. Really stellar.

She frowns as she digs through her purse. "Maybe two or three years ago, that was true—"

"It was true two weeks ago!" I sputter.

She stops. "What are you talking about?"

"Nothing. Never mind."

She shakes her head and pulls out another one of her protein shakes.

Let it go, Graham. I drum my fingers on the table and try to think of something else—*anything* else—but I only get more annoyed when she takes a big gulp of her shake and makes a face.

"Order some real food if that stuff's so terrible."

The family in the booth across from us stops what they're doing and looks over. I ignore them, but Sarah doesn't. She smiles and waves, then lowers her voice. "What the hell is wrong with you?"

"I don't like seeing you starve yourself. That's what's wrong with me."

"I'm not starving myself," she says. "I'm taking in three thousand calories a day to make up for all of my workouts and practices. I'm just taking in the *right* kind of calories—"

"Why didn't you order a regular salad then? Why a side?"

"Because I had a snack before you picked me up and I'm not that hungry."

"But you just said you were starving before we came in here."

"I guess I wasn't as hungry as I thought."

"Are you telling the truth?"

"YES!" The family looks over at us again, but Sarah doesn't seem to notice. "How do you expect me to become a professional ballerina if I don't learn to control what I put in my body? And how do you expect me to do it without the full support of my boyfriend who supposedly loves me?"

"Oh, so I just 'supposedly' love you now?"

"You know what I mean."

"I didn't think you even wanted to be a professional ballerina."

"What did you think I was going to do?"

"I thought you wanted to be a soccer mom and live in Christmas the rest of your life."

"Well, that would be kind of hard to do if I follow you to New York, now wouldn't it?" she yells.

"Who said I wanted to go to New York?" I shout back, matching her nearly-hysterical tone.

"YOU DID!"

She jumps to her feet, tugging her purse onto her shoulder. Every eye in the diner is on us now, and unlike a restaurant in a big city where the waiter might have asked us to keep it down or take it outside, everyone in here is practically salivating over our fight, trying to commit every word to memory so the rest of the town will know exactly what we said come breakfast.

Sarah glares at them all, then leans down and whispers, "I want you to think about something, Graham. I want you to think about the night you asked me if I'd follow you to New York. *You* were the one who said I was good enough to have a professional ballet career, not me. *You* were the one who asked me to imagine what our lives could be like, you with some big fancy job and me dancing in front of hundreds of people every night. You can't just plant that dream in my head and then take it away when you don't like the intense commitment it will take on my part to make it happen. So, I want you to think about that night long and hard and decide if you still want that for us. Okay?"

She turns on her heel and storms out before I can answer. The waiter reappears, setting down my plate, milkshake, Sarah's side salad, and the check.

"I would," I mumble as the rest of the diner's patrons

slowly turn back to their meals, "if I could remember it."

I take a bite out of my burger, but it tastes like sawdust. I pay the bill with cash, then head out to the car. Sarah's only made it a block down Main Street by the time I pull up next to her. I roll down the window and tell her to get in the car so I can take her home before she freezes to death. She gets in, but neither of us says a word.

For the first time since I made the wish, I go to bed half hoping I'll wake up tomorrow with everything back to normal. Sarah will be back with Jeremy, and I'll just be some loser whose biggest problem is finding a date to the dance. As miserable as old me was, it's got to be better than living a life where I don't know what's real and what isn't.

9

✳✳✳

No such luck.

The pictures of Sarah and me are still on the entryway table the next morning, and I can't tell if the sharp tug in my gut upon seeing them is disappointment or relief.

Relief. Definitely relief.

"Everything okay?" Mom asks as I get a bowl of cereal.

I shrug.

"Everything go all right with the float?"

"Yeah."

She taps her fingernails against her coffee mug. "You and Sarah have a fight?"

I glance up at her. "How do you do that?"

"It's a gift." She pulls out a chair at the breakfast table to sit across from me. "Spill."

"It was nothing, really. We just fought over those stupid diet shakes she's been drinking."

"Ah, I see."

"Well I'm glad somebody does," I snap.

She gives me a stern look.

"Sorry," I say. "I just . . ." I thought nothing would change. I thought Sarah and me being together would make things *less* complicated. I thought I would be happier than this. "I just don't like seeing her do something she doesn't want to do."

"You mean the diet?"

"Yeah."

"And how do you know she doesn't want to be on her diet?"

"Because she's always talking about how she's starving and how her diet's killing her, and then she makes a face like her protein shakes are the worst things she's ever tasted, but when I tell her to just eat a damn burger already—sorry, a burger already, she flips out on me."

"Being on a diet is hard work. I should know. I've tried every fad diet there is, and I've never once said, 'This diet is the best thing I've ever done. I'm not hungry at all.' But I did it anyway because I wasn't feeling like my healthiest self. And I'll do it again after Christmas because I've already gained five pounds in holiday weight since Thanksgiving. But *wanting* to do it doesn't mean it's not going to be difficult, and I'm not even trying to pursue something as rigorous as a professional ballet career."

"What are you saying?"

She rolls her eyes. "Sarah doesn't want you to tell her to eat a burger when she complains about her diet. She wants you to tell her how proud you are of her for doing something so difficult to pursue her dream. She wants you to tell her you could never do it and then make some silly promise, like: As soon as she's off her diet, you'll go to the bakery at six o'clock in the morning and eat a dozen hot doughnuts right out of the oven."

My brow arches. "Did Dad do that for you?"

She looks down at her coffee and smiles. "Oh yeah. It's become a bit of a tradition."

"But what if she doesn't want to be a professional ballerina? What if she's only doing it because I asked her to go to New York with me?"

Mom freezes. "Do you want to go to New York?"

"I don't know," I say. "I mean, I've always wanted to go to college in a big city, but that was because—" I stop myself before I can say *because I wanted to get away from Sarah* and double back. "Because, uh, I thought it would be an adventure or something. But I don't know if that's what Sarah wants."

"Have you asked her?"

"Kind of."

Mom's gaze sharpens.

"Okay, maybe I haven't asked her flat-out, but why would she go this far to do something she doesn't want to do?"

Mom leans back in her chair. "Love can make people do things they never dreamed of doing."

I glance at my untouched cereal. The corn flakes are soggy now, and the milk's turning yellow. "You really think she loves me?"

"Why else would she have hung around here the past two years? Talk to her. And eat your cereal before it disintegrates."

"Yes, ma'am."

***

Sarah isn't waiting for me outside her house to walk to school together, but I find her in front of her locker, talking to Jeremy. She's shaking her head and looking up at him as if he can fix whatever's broken between us. He's patting her shoulder and looking down at her like she's the most beautiful thing he's ever seen, and I don't know whether to feel jealous or guilty. Jeremy wraps his arms around her, and she leans her head into the crook of his neck. For a moment, it's like nothing's changed. Then Jeremy's gaze catches mine, and he lets her go, hiking his backpack up on his shoulder.

"Hey," I say.

Sarah looks down at her books.

"I'll just let you two talk," Jeremy says, backing away.

I smile at him to let him know everything's cool between us, but he doesn't return it.

My guilt-o-meter goes up a couple notches.

But that's stupid, right? I shouldn't feel guilty. Sarah and I were obviously meant to be together, or else the wish wouldn't have worked.

I lean against the locker next to Sarah's. "I'm really sorry about last night."

She freezes. "You are?"

"Yeah, I'm . . ." I think about what Mom said and take a deep breath. "I'm actually really proud of you. It takes a lot of dedication to stay on a diet like that, especially when your jerk of a boyfriend tries to eat a cheeseburger and a chocolate milkshake right in front of you."

She closes her locker. Her eyes are red and shiny, but her lips twitch up as she says, "I'm sorry too. I shouldn't have made such a scene."

I hold out my hand. "Truce?"

An image of Piper doing the same thing to me at the ice cream parlor floods my mind, and for a moment, she's all I see, with her blonde hair framed by a halo of Christmas lights and her eyes shining brighter than all of them combined.

Sarah swats my hand away and kisses me. "Truce."

I tell myself to kiss her back.

The warning bell rings. I use the distraction to break the

kiss and slip my arm around her.

"Want me to walk you to your locker?" she asks.

"Nah, I don't want you to be late to class. But could we talk later?"

"Is it going to be a bad talk or a good talk?"

"A good talk," I say. "Like the one we had about New York. A planning-for-the-future kind of talk."

"I'd like that," she says. "Text me, and we'll figure it out."

But when we check our schedules, it turns out we won't be able to get together until Friday night. I try to tell myself it's probably for the best, as it'll give me more time to figure out what the heck I actually want to do in the future, now that Sarah's in the picture. Do I really want to go to a big city? Or would I be happy going to William & Mary, like Sarah and Jeremy had planned?

Still, even though I appreciate the chance to think before we talk, I don't like that we're spending so much time away from each other—because we *are* drifting apart. I can feel it, but I don't know how to stop it, not while both of our schedules are keeping us so busy.

But the worst part of it all is I'd be lying if I said I didn't enjoy spending the time with Piper. We have a lot more in common than I would have thought, and even when we don't agree on something—like favorite movies or music or books—she somehow turns it around so that we're making fun of each other until we're both laughing so hard we're crying. The holiday rush isn't nearly as unbearable with the extra help at the bookstore either, and the float is even starting to resemble something other than a bunch of random crepe paper glued and stapled together.

"You got your outfit picked out for the dance?" Piper asks Thursday night as we pile papier-mâché books into Christmas tree shapes to resemble the one in the bookstore's display window, with spines sticking out to reveal each title in big, sparkly letters. This one's the children's book tree, so titles like *To Kill a Mockingbird* and *Tom Sawyer* and *Harry Potter* stick out from every angle. "I forgot to ask Jeremy if the guys wear tuxes, like prom, or if it's more informal."

"Suits for the winter formal," I say, "which makes it pretty easy, considering I only have one."

"You don't want to buy a new one?" she asks, climbing the stepladder to reach the top of the book tree.

"Why would I do that?"

She rolls her eyes and mutters, "*Men.*"

"What about you? You get a dress yet?"

She nods. "Queenie took me into Richmond to get it. I wanted something classic, but I wanted to be able to dance in it too, you know?"

"Not really," I say, "but I'll take your word for it." And then one word sticks out in my head, and I smack my hand against my face. "Dance."

"Huh?"

"*Dance!*"

"You keep saying that word like it should mean something, but—"

"I don't know how to dance."

"Wait a second," she says. "You're taking a ballerina—a girl who has devoted her *entire* life to busting a move—to the winter formal, and you don't know how to dance?"

"I think I'm going to be sick."

"Oh, don't be so dramatic." Her glue gun clatters on the floor, and the stepladder creaks as she climbs off. "I can teach you."

"You can?"

"You're not going to be competing in any ballroom dance competitions, but I can teach you a basic box step for slow dances and a couple general moves for the fast stuff." She switches the radio station to Top Forty and cranks up the volume. "But first, you need to show me what you've got."

"Ha ha, very funny."

She crosses her arms over her chest.

"Wait, are you serious?"

"Would you stop being such a baby and start dancing already? I can't help you if you don't show me what I'm working with."

I crack my knuckles. "Okay, but don't laugh."

"I won't."

"And don't make fun of me."

She mimes locking her lips and throwing away the key.

"And don't watch me."

She puts her hands on her hips.

"Okay, okay," I say. "Here goes nothing."

I listen to the music for a second, trying to catch the beat. I'm not terrible with rhythm. I can clap along in church just fine, and I even took some piano lessons when I was younger, although I'm not sure that's going to help me much considering the metronome always distracted me—crap, I lost the beat already.

I close my eyes and clear my mind, then start bobbing my head to the downbeat. I sway my body from side to side, doing some kind of weird horizontal fist pump. I think I even throw in a Macarena move or two. I'm about to go into the one move my cousin taught me—the running man—when Piper claps her hands, and I open my eyes.

"Not bad," she says. "Granted, I think Sarah would prefer it if you had your eyes open and if you moved your feet a bit, but we can work on that. You have good rhythm, and that's a hard thing to teach."

"Oh good. So at least I'm not a total failure."

She smiles, then takes my hands and places them on her hips. Alarm bells start blaring in my head.

"What are you doing?"

"Nothing dirty, I promise," she says as if it were the far-thest thought from her mind. "All of your movement starts in your hips. You want to move them to the beat." She starts swinging her hips side to side, and my throat suddenly feels like I downed a gallon of peroxide.

"I, uh, thought I did that," I say.

She puts pressure on my hips, making them move in time with hers. "You were doing more of a full body sway, which didn't look horrible if you were actually going for the drunk and off-balance look. Were you?"

I shake my head.

"That's what I thought. Okay, I'm going to let go now, but I want you to keep moving your hips to the beat." She takes a step back and I try to keep moving my hips, but it suddenly feels awkward and unnatural without the pres-sure of her palms guiding me.

"I don't think a man's body is supposed to move like this," I mutter.

"Nonsense. People have been dancing since the dawn of time. It's one of the most natural forms of self-expression there is."

"I'm pretty sure all I'm expressing right now is that I look like a human washing machine."

"I swear you don't. *This* is the washing machine." She puts her hands on her hips and pivots on her heels, moving her hips in a wide circle as she spins.

In response, I go into a full-blown coughing fit.

"You okay?" she asks.

"Allergies," I croak.

She smirks. "Okay, now here's another trick to dancing. To swing your hips better, you need to let the movement glide from your hips and into your thighs, down your knees, and back up. They should all be working together, and it helps if you take a wider stance and bend your knees a little.

You sure you're okay?"

"Yeah," I say, coughing again. "Just a tickle in my throat."

I spread my feet like she shows me and bend my knees with the beat too.

"I feel like a Stormtrooper."

She laughs. "Okay, so you're a little stiff—"

"*A little?*"

"You're just self-conscious. You can't think about what you look like or what other people think of you when you dance."

"Easy to say if your date's not training to be a professional ballerina," I grit through my teeth.

"Okay, so let me ask you this: Do you think your ballerina girlfriend would rather watch other people dance all night because her boyfriend is too worried about what he looks like, or do you think she might actually want to have some fun?"

"Touché."

"Here. Watch me for a second."

"Why?"

"Because I'm going to show you that it's okay to be goofy when you dance. The most important thing is to have fun."

A pop song with a fast beat comes on, and Piper throws up her hands and starts rolling her body with the music. I try not to notice her curves as her back arches and her hips swing like a pendulum. She's not even trying to be sexy— she's just lost in the music, letting her body move, and that makes it even sexier.

Think of Sarah. Think of Sarah.

Better yet, think of Grandma.

"Open your eyes!" Piper yells over the music. "You're going to miss the best part."

I look up at her as the chorus pumps through the speakers. She plants her feet like she's about to throw down some seriously complicated move I could never replicate in a thousand years, puts one hand behind her neck, and—

Does the sprinkler.

I laugh. "Wow. Now that's sexy."

She stops, her brows arched, and I clamp my mouth shut.

"If you think *that's* sexy," she says, grinning, "just wait until you see this." She holds out her hands in front of her and does the shopping cart.

"Hey, let me get in on that," I say, pushing my own invisible cart and placing imaginary items inside.

Before I know it, we're doing every cheesy dance move ever created.

"See?" She shouts as she goes full *Flashdance*, pumping her legs up and down and shaking her head. "Dancing's fun!"

I try to do a moonwalk and trip over my laces. Piper's hands grip my shoulders, steadying me.

"Yeah, okay," I say, laughing. "Dancing's fun."

The song fades, and the DJ says, "We've got a special request to take it *way* back to a classic slow song for all you lovers out there tonight."

Piper clears her throat as the song starts—a ballad Patrick Swayze sang in *Dirty Dancing*. "Okay. You, um, ready to slow dance?"

"Uh, yeah. Sure."

She takes a step forward. "So, there are obviously a lot of ways to slow dance, but since we're talking about a high school dance here, we'll just stick with the basic my-arms-around-your-neck-and-your-arms-around-my-waist maneuver. Sound good?"

I try not to sound too eager as I say, "Yeah. Sounds good."

Her arms slide around my neck, and I place my hands at her waist, just barely touching her.

"Is this right?" I ask.

She nods.

She's so close, I can feel the warmth of her breath against my neck. She looks up at me from beneath her lashes, and everything else fades away.

"You can hold me a little tighter," she says. "If you want."

"O-okay."

"And now we just kind of sway back and forth," she says, her voice barely a whisper.

The air seems to thicken around us. I stare into her eyes, gray like a storm cloud, and she stares back. The tip of her nose brushes my chin as she moves closer. I can't think. Can't speak. Can't do anything but lean in, my forehead brushing hers.

Her breath comes faster now as her hands move from my neck down to my chest. I reach up and grab one of her hands in mine, my own breath shallow.

"What are we doing?" she asks.

"I don't know."

She tips her head back, and I've never wanted anything more than to kiss her here, in this old barn, illuminated by the warm glow of old-fashioned light bulbs dangling like stars on strings, the pulse of the music wrapping around us and the winter wind howling outside and my heart ramming so hard against my ribs, I'm sure she can hear it over everything else.

Instead, I let go of her hand and take a step back.

"Piper—"

"I'm sorry," she says, her face in her hands. "Oh God, I'm so sorry. I don't know what came over me. You have a girlfriend and—and I should go."

My brow furrows. "You don't have to go—"

She shakes her head and grabs her purse. "It's getting late. I'll call Queenie to pick me up, and I can start walking—"

"Don't be ridiculous. I'm taking you home."

She stares at her shoes as I grab my things, and I want to

tell her it wasn't just her, that I wanted to kiss her in a way I've never wanted to kiss anyone before—not even Sarah. With Sarah, it was always more about wondering what it would be like to kiss her, mixed with the jealousy that Jeremy got to do it every day. But with Piper, the need to kiss her was primal. I needed to be closer to her, to press my lips against hers, to breathe her in. Even now, being this far away from her is physically painful, tensing up my entire body and tightening my chest with the need to get closer, to wrap my arms around her and just *be*.

But I can't tell her any of that. I have a girlfriend. And not just any girl—*the* girl.

I'm just confused, I tell myself as we get into the car, still not speaking. I can't be falling for Piper. We can't be meant for each other, because if I was meant to be with Piper, and Jeremy was meant to be with Sarah, then this would have never happened. My wish would have never come true.

Before I know it, I'm pulling up to her house. The seatbelt clicks as she releases it.

"Can we just forget this ever happened?" she asks.

My grip tightens on the steering wheel. "Is that what you want?"

She frowns. "I don't know what I want." She takes a deep breath and closes her eyes. "But I do know if we don't forget about this, it's going to be impossible to work together. I'm going to feel weird around you and you're going to feel weird around me, and I don't want that. I really like you, Graham. You're a good friend. I don't want to lose you."

There it is again, the word *friend* coming from the lips of a girl I'm falling in love with, but it hurts even worse this time, because it isn't my pride she's hurting, like it was with Sarah, but something else. Something deeper.

"You're not going to lose me," I say. The words feel like

sludge in my mouth. "It's already forgotten."

She sighs. "Thank you." She clambers out of the car, then looks back at me. "See you tomorrow?"

"Yeah," I say. "See you."

I wait until she gets inside, then put the car in drive and head for home. Sarah's bedroom light is on, but when I get to my room, I close the blinds and keep the lights off. I don't want to talk to her right now, not when my thoughts are swirling like a tilt-a-whirl, circling back to Piper and jasmine perfume and a slow song I'd heard before but never really understood until now.

When I do finally fall asleep, Piper follows me into my dreams. She tells me we can't be together.

"Why?" I ask, my voice echoing around us.

"Because," she says, "you didn't wish for me."

10

***

Things are weird at the bookstore the next day, despite our conversation in the car. Piper barely says two words to me, and when she does, she's overly professional and distant. For my part, I try not to pay any attention to her, for fear that whatever part of my brain keeps trying to sabotage my relationship with Sarah will take over, but my gaze keeps zeroing in on the slightest of movements. The bend in her fingers around her coffee thermos. The tiny wisps of white-blonde hair circling her ear. The slight crinkling around her eyes when she smiles at customers. The chewing of her bottom lip as she covertly opens a new book behind the counter and starts reading.

Things are also weird because, no matter how far away from each other we try to stay, we somehow keep bumping into each other. It's like we're so distracted with not looking at each other or thinking about what happened last night that we aren't really paying attention to what we're doing. I bump into her in the travel section, sending the books in her hands flying. She thwacks into me as she comes around the corner into the history section. On and on it goes, until I'm certain I'm going to wake up tomorrow covered in bruises.

And then, at the end of the shift, with both of us behind the counter as Piper rings up the last customers and as I go over inventory, we keep reaching for the same things—same pen, same clipboard, same candy cane off the tree—our fingers brushing and tangling with every move.

"Sorry," I mutter for what feels like the thousandth time when I reach for the keys at the same time she does. "You want to lock up?"

"No, it's okay. You go ahead."

I take the key off the hook and try to sound casual—and fail miserably—as I ask, "Any plans tonight?"

"Um, yeah, actually. I'm going out with Jeremy."

I whirl around. "You are?"

"He texted me last night after you dropped me off," she says, a blush creeping into her cheeks. "He thought we should get together before the dance. Hang out just the two of us. And I agreed."

"Why? I mean"—I shake my head—"that sounds . . . fun."

"Yeah," she says. "I think it will be. It was kind of hard for us to get to know each other on a double date to the movies like that, especially when the other couple was you and Sarah."

"What's that supposed to mean? *Especially* when it was me and Sarah?"

Her lips thin. "Nothing. I just meant, well . . . you, Sarah, and Jeremy grew up together, so it's kind of hard for me to integrate myself into that." She picks up a stack of books she's been looking over and disappears behind a shelf.

Something about the way she said it—*especially* me and Sarah—makes me think there's more to it than that, but I decide not to push it. Instead, I ask, "What does Bookstore Boy think about you two going out?"

Piper's head pokes out. "*Jordan* and I are just casually dating right now whenever he's in town. Besides, Jeremy and I aren't really 'going out'. We just want to get to know each other better before the dance."

"Oh."

She reappears, grabbing her coat and purse from behind the counter. "How about you? Doing anything with Sarah tonight?"

"Yeah, we'll probably watch a movie or something."

"Good. That sounds . . . fun," she says, mimicking me.

"Yeah. It does."

So why does it sound like a funeral dirge when I say it?

I wait for her to join me at the door before turning off the lights. A soft, yellow glow streams in through the display window from the old-fashioned lampposts outside, gilding Piper's cheek amber gold in the darkness.

I force my gaze away and open the door. "Ladies first."

She steps through the door and I follow, locking it behind me.

"See you tomorrow," she says, starting down the sidewalk.

"I'll be the one in the suit," I call after her.

She laughs.

I watch her walk away, her ponytail swinging with every step, then shove my hands in my pockets and start for home.

Sarah's already in the kitchen with my mom when I get there, helping her bake a chocolate sheet cake with crushed peppermint frosting on top. Sarah swirls her finger through the mixing bowl and licks a large dollop of chocolate batter off her finger.

"What about your diet?" I ask.

She smirks. "I'm still on it, but you helped me realize it's important to cut myself some slack every once in a while.

Speaking of." She hops off her stool and grabs her purse from the corner of the room, pulling out a box of Milk Duds. "I brought these over for our movie tonight."

And there she is, a glimmer of the girl I fell in love with. I don't say anything. I just wrap her in a big hug, and she laughs.

"You seem disproportionally excited about this," she says. "I mean, I know they're the best candy in the world, but—"

"I just missed you." I give her one last squeeze and let go, ignoring the wide-eyed stares Sarah and Mom are giving me as I lean across the kitchen island. "Anything I can do to help?"

They set me to work making the salad for dinner while Sarah throws a box of spaghetti into a pot of boiling water and Mom rolls the meatballs on a sheet pan.

After dinner, Mom and Dad head upstairs, giving us the family room. Flames crackle in the fireplace, and all the lights have been turned off except for the white twinkle lights circling the tree.

"What movie do you want to watch?" she asks.

"I was actually hoping we could have that talk first," I say, holding out my hand. "Come here."

She takes my hand and settles herself on top of me, curling her knees to her chest and resting her arm on the pillow behind me. "Okay. Let's talk."

I take a deep breath. All of the thoughts that have been keeping me up at night collide into one another as I try to form a coherent sentence. "I've been thinking about our futures a lot lately. How long ago did we have that talk about moving to New York?"

She gives me a funny look but answers anyway. "A little over a year ago."

"I guess I've just been wondering if we weren't a little hasty, planning out the rest of our lives like that when we were only, what, fifteen?"

"Where are you going with this, Graham?"

A lock of hair falls across her cheek, and I push it behind her ear. "I want to make a new plan with you, but this time, I want to know what you really want."

She fidgets, pulling herself off of me and onto the cushion. "What do you mean?"

"I mean, take me out of the equation," I say, swallowing. "I want to know what you really want for yourself without worrying about how I fit into it."

"Are you breaking up with me?"

"No!" I take a deep breath. "No. I just want to make sure you get to do what you really want to with your life. If dancing for a professional ballet company is what you *really* want to do, I will support you one hundred percent. I'm serious. I will never give you crap about your diet again, and I'll even do my best to eat healthy when I'm around you so I'm not a bad influence. And when the holiday season is over, I'll go to all of your practices and I won't miss a single recital and I'll do everything in my power to help you make your dream come true. But if there's something else you want, just tell me, and I'll support that too."

"You really mean that?"

"Yeah. I do."

She looks away from me. "That's really sweet of you, but the truth is, I don't know *what* I want to do with my life. When I try to envision myself five or ten years from now, there's nothing. I draw a complete blank, and I just feel, I don't know, kind of . . . lost. So, when we had that conversation about New York, I grabbed onto it and ran with it because I *finally* had some kind of direction, something to work toward. But now you're changing your mind," she says, tears glistening in her eyes, "and that scares me because suddenly I don't have a plan anymore."

"Sarah." I wrap my arms around her, and she sobs into my shoulder. Was she like this with Jeremy? Did she not know what she wanted to do? She had seemed so sure of herself and her future with him, but maybe she's always been lost.

Or maybe she's just lost because she's with me.

I shove the thought aside, mostly because I don't have the answer to it, and it's not helping matters anyway. She's with me now, and there's a reason we're together—there has to be. A whole town full of people's lives wouldn't have changed just for us to be together if we weren't meant to be.

"How about we do this," I say, running my hands through her hair. "How about we put New York on hold for now, just until we figure out what we want to do?"

She pulls away from me, wiping her eyes. Mascara smudges onto her cheeks and fingers. "We have less than a year until we have to start applying to colleges. What if we don't figure it out by then?"

"We'll do what everyone else does. Go somewhere with a lot of majors and hope we figure it out before we graduate."

She makes a strangled sound that's part sob, part laugh. "Okay. Just . . . promise me something?"

"Anything."

"Promise we'll still be together by then. That way if we don't figure it out, at least we'll be lost together."

I press my lips to her temple. "Of course."

It's an easy promise to make because it's always been her and me. Ever since she moved in next door, and even after she and Jeremy started dating. I don't know what I've been doing with Piper or why I've been so attracted to her. I don't know if she's some sort of test I have to pass to keep the wish going or if I'm just a closet masochist, subconsciously sabotaging myself now that I finally have everything I've ever wanted. But the point is Sarah and I have been in each other's lives since we were kids and I can't imagine my life without her. Even when I was planning to move to a big city to get away from her, I knew I'd eventually find my way back to her. The time away was only meant for me to find some way to be okay with just being her friend.

Either way, Sarah is meant to be in my life and I'm meant to be in hers.

I wipe her tears away as she looks up at me with those Bambi-wide eyes. "You want to watch that movie now?"

"Let me just go clean myself up," she says, gesturing to the watery mascara lining her cheeks.

She disappears into the bathroom while I put a bag of popcorn in the microwave and pick *Christmas Vacation* on our streaming service. Not once does my mind wander to Piper for the rest of the night. At least, not until the end credits roll on the movie, when I'm shrugging into my coat to walk Sarah home and she says, "I hope Jeremy and Piper had fun tonight."

I pause, my coat halfway on. "Jeremy told you they were going out?"

"He didn't so much tell me as ask me."

"Why would he do that?"

She shrugs. "He just wanted to know if I thought they should get to know each other before the dance tomorrow night, that way things wouldn't be so awkward. I said it sounded like a good idea."

I follow Sarah through the door, and we start down the walkway toward her house. "You, um, talk to Jeremy often?"

She looks back at me. "You know I do. He's one of my best friends."

"Oh."

She smirks.

"What?"

"You're jealous."

"No, I'm not."

"It's okay," she says, wrapping her arms around my neck. "It makes us even, since I've been so jealous of Piper."

My brow arches. "Is that why you said it sounded like a good idea? Because you're still worried about Piper and me?"

"No," she says, "but that is an added bonus."

She kisses me good night before I can say anything else.

"Don't forget the carriage is picking us up at six tomorrow night for dinner, so you should head over here around five-thirty for pictures."

"I'll be here."

She disappears inside and shuts the door, and then it hits me in a way it hasn't before.

I am taking Sarah Clarke to the dance.

Just two weeks ago I was scouring my yearbook with a black marker like a total creeper, and now I'm taking Sarah to the dance.

I can't stop smiling. The thought stays with me until my head hits the pillow.

I'm taking Sarah to the dance.

I'm taking *Sarah* to the dance.

"Thank you, God," I whisper into the quiet, just before exhaustion takes over and I slip into a blessedly dreamless sleep.

Piper and I only work half a day at the bookstore. Aunt Bee lets us both go home early to get ready for the dance. Even after taking an extra-long shower, I have a full two hours with nothing to do, so I help Mom wrap presents in the dining room, my hands shaking so badly that each piece of wrapping paper I cut looks like it was mauled by a vicious dog.

"Why are you so nervous?" Mom asks, grabbing the scissors out of my hand. "It's not like this is your first dance."

She goes back to wrapping presents without a second thought and, just for a moment, I wish she knew.

Don't get me wrong, I was never a big fan of the way she went into Smother Mode whenever she'd notice me pining after Sarah, but I don't care how big of a baby it makes me sound, I could really use my mom right now. Granted, if she knew this really was my first dance, I'd have to put up with her taking a million pictures of me putting gel in my hair and tying my tie and probably even of me eating that bowl of cereal I had half an hour ago to tide me over until dinner, but she would also give me that comforting Mom look, the one that says everything's going to be okay, and I don't know if it would really make me feel better but at least I'd know someone understood.

Before I can stop myself, I blurt, "Mom?"

She looks up, her finger holding down the center of an untied bow. "Hmm?"

"I, uh . . ." But what am I supposed to say? That this actually *is* my first dance and I haven't really been dating Sarah that long, and I'm scared I'm going to mess everything up by running out of things to talk about before we even get to dessert, and then I'll terrify her with my horrid dance moves, and the entire night will be ruined?

"Did you, uh, do any of my laundry today?"

Her brow arches. "Everything's already folded and put away, and I hung up your suit on your bedroom door."

"Okay. Thanks."

"I'm more than a laundry maid, you know," she says, expertly tying a bow and curling the ends of the ribbon with the scissors.

"Believe me, I know."

She bops me on the nose with the tape dispenser.

I change into my suit at five. It's of the fitted black variety, and I throw on a black shirt and a red tie with it. I run some gel through my hair and try to make it look somewhat decent. A dollop of cologne later and I'm standing on Sarah's porch, knocking on her door.

Her dad answers.

"Hey, Mr. Clarke—"

"Come in," he says gruffly, his eyes narrowed.

"Okay."

He closes the door behind me and crosses his arms over his chest. "Sarah will be down in a minute."

"Good. That's, uh, good."

We stand in the entryway in an awkward silence as the grandfather clock next to the stairs *tick-tick-ticks.*

"I'm shocked you weren't late," he says, running his fingers over his mustache. "I've never seen someone move so slow in my life."

My brow furrows. "When? Just now?"

"No. At the toy drive."

"Oh."

"You still haven't apologized for that, you know."

"I didn't realize your family took it so seriously."

"And if you had, you would have run faster?"

Say yes. Say yes.

"Not really."

"Oh?" Mr. Clarke takes a step forward. "So, you have no respect for our family traditions, then?"

"It's just a contest, Mr. Clarke, and you won anyway."

"Yeah," he barks. "No thanks to you."

"Daddy," Sarah's voice drifts down the staircase. "Leave him alone."

I look up. She's wearing the silver dress she showed me in Riddle's Bridal the night I made the wish. It clings to her like a second skin, rippling down the curves of her body, and suddenly I forget what Mr. Clarke and I had been talking about. Her hair is up in some complicated, twisting knot, and her eyes and cheekbones shimmer with a silvery powder that makes her look a snow queen, delicate and beautiful—and slightly intimidating in an unattainable sort of way. But then she gives me the same warm smile she used to give Jeremy, and I remind myself she isn't unattainable anymore.

"You look beautiful," I tell her as she reaches the bottom step.

Mr. Clarke rolls his eyes at me, then gives Sarah a kiss on

her cheek. A smudge of silver powder clings to his lips, but I don't dare laugh. "Have a great time, sweetheart. And you," he says, glaring at me, "behave yourself."

"Always," I say.

He gives me a look that clearly says he doesn't believe me, then stalks off into the other room.

Mrs. Clarke comes down the stairs behind her daughter, flashing her phone. "Okay," she says, "let's get some pictures in front of the fireplace there . . ."

Half an hour later, the horse-drawn carriage arrives. I argued against its impracticability when Sarah first mentioned it, since we'll have to call our parents to pick us up after the dance, but it only took the barest fluttering of Sarah's lashes to change my mind.

Mrs. Clarke continues to take pictures as I help Sarah into the carriage, and then we're clip-clopping down the street, a red-and-green tartan blanket spread over our laps. I put my arm around Sarah as the darkened sky opens up and large, fluffy snowflakes begin to fall like wisps of cotton. Halos of yellow light dapple the street from the old-fashioned lampposts, each hung with a fragrant wreath.

"Warm enough?" I ask as Sarah leans her head on my shoulder.

She nods. "Sorry about my dad."

"It's no big deal."

"It is," she says. "I know it bothers you, but if you just give him some time, there's no way he won't like you."

I don't say anything, because all I can think to say is that he liked Jeremy from the start, and that he liked me well enough when I was just the dorky kid next door who couldn't get a date, but now that I'm dating his daughter, he can't stand the sight of me.

We pull up to Piper's house. Jeremy's already here, and

they're standing on the porch while Queenie takes pictures of them. Piper waves as she spots us over her grandma's shoulder, and I suddenly stop breathing.

I vaguely register what Piper is wearing—a dark-green sleeveless dress, which poofs out in a bell shape from her waist and hits just below her knees—and how different her hair looks, curled like a 1950s movie star, but it's more the way she looks at me, her eyes brighter than this entire Christmas-crazed town, that socks me in the gut, punching every ounce of air from my lungs.

Sarah clears her throat, and it's only then that I realize I'm in an awkward half-sitting, half-standing position in the carriage. I wave at Piper and Jeremy as they get closer, as if that is what I meant to do all along.

"You guys ready to boogie?" I ask them.

"You know it," Piper says. I reach out my hand to help her into the carriage. Electricity sparks up my arm as she takes it, and our eyes lock, and then, much too soon, her hand slides from mine, and she sits down next to Jeremy.

"Sarah," Jeremy says as the carriage starts, her name hushed on his lips. "You look beautiful."

She blushes. "Thank you." But she's still side-eying me.

Dinner isn't much better. We barely talk through the salad course. It helps that there's a jazz band in the corner of the small café playing instrumental Christmas music. At least it makes the tension less obvious.

By the time our main courses arrive, Jeremy and Sarah are talking about the new album from a band I've never heard of, and it doesn't seem like Piper has either. Piper alternates between cutting up her steak and watching the jazz players as they talk. She glances at me, and I know I should be embarrassed to be caught staring at her, but I can't look away.

"You look really nice," she says, her lips curving into her

signature half smile. The dim mood lighting catches in the strands of her hair and bounces off her skin, softening her around the edges like a mirage. "That's a great suit."

I clear my throat. "You look, um . . ." Radiant. Stunning. Gorgeous. Like a dream prayed into life. "Really nice too."

I expect Sarah to look over at me, to interrupt us, but she's so intent on her conversation with Jeremy, she doesn't even notice me.

"Thanks." Piper glances at Sarah and Jeremy too, now bent even closer to each other and laughing as if they've never heard anything as funny as whatever joke one of them just said. She leans across the table and whispers, "You ready to dance?"

"I think so." The words come out more breathless than I intended as I remember the feeling of Piper in my arms. Warm and soft and absolutely mesmerizing.

"Just remember to have fun," she murmurs. "And don't move too much during the slow dance so you don't step on her feet."

"God forbid," I whisper back. "Those things should be insured."

"What should be insured?" Sarah asks, suddenly looking at Piper and me, all trace of humor gone from her face.

The look she gives me is pure suspicion.

I laugh it off. "Your feet. Piper told me to take it easy during the slow dances so I don't step on them. I can't be responsible for ruining the feet of a future ballet star."

"Oh." Sarah smiles and shakes her head slightly, like she was being ridiculous suspecting us. My heart squeezes in my chest because she wasn't being ridiculous. I don't know what's going on with me. I don't know how I can be thinking about Piper when my dream girl—the girl I wished for—is sitting right next to me.

Is it self-sabotage? Do I, on some deep level, not want

to be happy?

You shouldn't feel bad. Sarah's flirting with Jeremy right in front of you.

I shove that thought out of my mind as forcefully as it entered. She's not flirting with him. They're friends. Like Sarah and I were.

Aren't they?

"Well, speaking of my feet," Sarah says, "I have some news."

I lean forward. "Do tell."

"Madame made it official today. I'm going to play Clara on the *Nutcracker* float."

"Sarah!" Jeremy nearly shouts, his grin so wide, I'm afraid his face is about to split in two. "That's amazing!"

"And that's not all," she says, beaming at Jeremy before looking back at me. "Madame has a friend on the board of admissions at Juilliard, and she invited him to the parade. He's going to be front and center in front of city hall when we stop to give our performance." She grabs my hand. "This could be it. All of our plans could come true because of this."

I force a smile and squeeze her hand. "That's incredible, babe. I'm so proud of you."

I lean forward and kiss her—because I am proud, but mostly because I am guilty. Sarah's fighting for our future, the future we decided on together—even if I don't remember it—and meanwhile I'm too busy thinking about Piper and worrying about Jeremy to focus on what we have.

She kisses me back, a quick peck, as she jumps up and down a little in her seat. "I don't know about you guys, but I think this news calls for dessert."

This time, my smile is not forced. "There's my girl."

I kiss her one more time. I don't miss the look Jeremy gives her, the one of pain and longing I used to wear all the time, and I don't miss the way Piper's shoulders tense and her eyes shutter, as if a physical wall has gone up, separating her from me.

It's for the best. I have to stop leading her on. I'm with Sarah, and that's the way it's meant to be. The way it *has* to be. Or else everything changed for nothing.

I love her, I think, squeezing Sarah's hand one more time. *I love her, I love her, I love her.*

I just wish it sounded more like a reminder and less like I'm still trying to convince myself.

✳ ✳ ✳

12

***

Piper breaks off from our group to go talk to her cheer-leader friends when we get to the dance. She angles her head toward Jeremy, a clear invitation for him to come with her, but he stays with us. Piper doesn't seem fazed by it, but I nudge him in the side anyway.

"Dude, that's your date. Shouldn't you hang out with her?"

He shrugs. "I'll catch up with her later. Besides, it's not like we're a thing. We're not even close friends."

"You're a real prince, you know that?" The words come out like a joke, but I'm not sure I meant them that way.

Sarah laughs, and Jeremy rolls his eyes.

"Graham's right," she tells him. "You should ask her to dance."

"It's not like every other guy in here isn't going to."

Sarah gives him a look.

He sighs. "Fine. I'll be back."

He takes a deep breath and crosses the room to Piper, hands in his pockets. She nods at his request, a smile lighting her face, and leads him to the dance floor as the song switches from Frank Sinatra to Michael Bublé.

"Do you think they're going to play Christmas music all night?" I ask, not sure if I know how to dance to "O Holy Night", but judging by the fake snowflakes and Christmas decorations strung throughout the gym, I'm going to need to figure it out.

"They switch to Top Forty after Bublé," Sarah answers. "Don't you remember last year?"

"Oh yeah." I clear my throat. "I forgot."

"You've been doing that a lot lately. Are you sure everything's okay?"

"Yeah. Just a lot on my mind."

"Us?"

I put my arm around her. "Sometimes, but only in the best way. Want to dance?"

"I thought you'd never ask."

When I take Sarah into my arms, I don't think about Piper in a fuzzy white sweater in a dusty old barn, the scent of pine needles and jasmine perfume thick around us, her gray eyes deep and vibrant as a storm-wrenched sea. I don't think about her body pressed against mine, her breath fanning my neck, or the sudden desire I felt to run the pad of my thumb over her bottom lip.

I focus on Sarah and don't think about Piper at all.

✹✹✹

"All right, y'all. You know what time it is," Trey Garner says into a mic onstage. "It's time to crown our Christmas king and queen."

"Did you forget about this too?" Sarah, asks, laughing at my shocked expression as everyone moves closer to the stage.

"Uh, yeah. Kind of." Although I don't know how I could have. Sarah got it last year, and I bet she's a shoo-in for it again. I don't remember who got king, and I have no clue who will get it this year. One of the jocks, probably.

Definitely not me.

First, Trey names the members of the court. Sarah goes up with a couple cheerleaders and the class president. I catch Piper's eye, and she shrugs like, *Can't win them all.*

I wink at her before I can stop myself, and her smile fades.

I clear my throat and focus my attention back on the stage, where four of the five guys have already been called. One quarterback, one point guard, one running back, the kid who played the lead in last year's spring musical, and—

"Jeremy Davis!"

Jeremy grins sheepishly and walks onstage, his wrestling buddies clapping him on the back and the crowd going wild while I stand there, my mouth agape. Old gamer Jeremy wouldn't have been seen anywhere near that stage except to cheer Sarah on, let alone be called up as a member of the court, but apparently new Jeremy isn't just a wrestler—he's also a really popular one.

"Get it, Jeremy!" someone shouts.

How did I not notice this before?

Because every time you saw Jeremy, you were with Sarah, or talking about Sarah, and it didn't matter how many people were around him, how many people had been talking to him, because he suddenly looked all alone in the world.

But this is a better life for him, right? I mean, I've never been popular, but the movies all make it seem like it's the pinnacle anyone could hope to achieve. So, yeah, he doesn't have Sarah anymore, but at least he's not in the shadows anymore either.

You're just trying to soothe a guilty conscience.

Yeah, and I'm going to be doing it for the rest of my life.

Careful. You're starting to sound ungrateful.

Not ungrateful. Just . . . uncertain.

But you love Sarah.

I do.

You always have.

I know.

So why doesn't it feel right?

"All right, here we go," Trey says, holding up an envelope. "This year's Christmas king and queen are . . . Jeremy Davis and Sarah Clarke!"

The whole room goes wild as Trey puts the crowns on Jeremy and Sarah's heads.

"Now the king and queen will lead us in a dance."

Jeremy looks at Sarah and offers her his hand. She blushes and takes it. A couple people whistle as others clap. It's only as I watch them descend the stairs and into the ring of space the crowd has made for them that I realize my hands have been in my pockets this whole time.

I haven't clapped or cheered once.

The music starts, a slow romantic song. Jeremy continues to hold Sarah's right hand, wrapping his other hand around her waist. He looks down at her, and she looks up at him.

They don't take their eyes off each other.

"Oh, don't they just look perfect together," one of the chaperones says behind me. I turn to glare at her, the freshman English teacher, but she doesn't even notice me.

"Are they dating?" another chaperone—a mom—asks.

"No, but look at them. You can't deny there's something there."

I tear my eyes away from the women and glance back at Sarah and Jeremy. He's whispering something to her now, his head bent low to her ear. Her fingers clench his suit jacket like she doesn't want to let go.

Even here, even after the wish, even in a world where

she's only ever been mine, all anyone sees is that Jeremy and Sarah are perfect for each other.

Trey invites other couples to join the dance as the chorus picks up again. I still haven't moved.

A tap on my shoulder.

I turn.

"You looked a little lonely over here," Piper says. "Want to dance?"

And even though I know I shouldn't, the look she gives me makes me think she sees it too, the way Sarah and Jeremy gravitate toward each other, an unstoppable force.

I nod and take her hand, leading her onto the dance floor. My eyes are on Jeremy and Sarah, but my focus is on the feeling of Piper's skin against mine, the way it shoots sparks up and down my arm.

You're being tested, I think. To make sure you deserve the wish. That has to be what this is.

So why, even when I'm confused and my heart is breaking, does nothing feel more real in my entire world—more *right*—than Piper's hand cupped in mine?

I swallow as I turn toward her.

"Simple box step," she says, putting her arms around my neck. "Nothing fancy. I don't need to go to the hospital tonight."

"Ha," I say, putting my arms around her waist.

"I'm just trying to make you laugh. I saw the way you were looking at them."

"Thanks."

Her eyes meet mine. "She loves you, you know."

"Everyone thinks she should be with Jeremy."

"What do you think?"

I feel the old Graham stirring inside of me, the one who never understood Sarah and Jeremy's relationship, the one that felt like he could make Sarah happier if only given the chance, and I want to shout that they're wrong, but when I look at Piper, everything gets blurry.

Old Graham feels like a jerk who didn't really know anything at all.

"I don't know."

I pull Piper closer as the song goes to the bridge, and she holds me tighter. The crowd starts to fade away, blurring at the edges, until all I can see—all I *want* to see—is Piper.

You're falling in love with her.

No.

You are.

I can't be.

That doesn't change the fact that you are.

Piper's lips part as she stares up at me, her eyes searching mine, and I do what I wanted to do in the barn. I rub the pad of my thumb across her lower lip.

She exhales sharply and takes a step back, her arms looser around my neck. "Why did you do that?"

"I don't know that either."

Lie.

"Graham," she says, my name a breath on her lips, "I—"

The crowd gasps. I turn toward the source of the noise and see Sarah running away from Jeremy.

Jeremy runs after her, and all I can think is, *She saw.*

She saw me with Piper.

She saw me wanting to kiss Piper. It had to have been written all over my face.

And then all I can think is, It's over.

And it feels like my world's tilting sideways.

13

***

The music in the gym fades as I run out into the dark, locker-lined hallway. I pull up short at the sight of Jeremy comforting Sarah, holding her hand and gently brushing the tears from her cheeks.

"Sarah," he says, with more pain and longing in his voice than I knew a person could hold. "I know you love me too."

"Jeremy, don't."

"Say it, then. Say you don't love me."

She chokes out a sob. "I can't."

"Why?" He pushes her hair behind her ears and tilts her chin up to meet his gaze. "Tell me."

Sarah closes her eyes.

I step out of the shadows. "I'd like to hear the answer to that myself."

She takes a step back, away from Jeremy. "Graham."

Jeremy thrusts his hands in his pockets and barely meets my gaze. He starts to say something, but I hold up a hand.

"Sarah?" I ask.

There's a weird tone to my voice. I don't know what to make of it. There's hurt there, seeing her with Jeremy, knowing that, even here, even when everything has changed for us to be together, she's still drawn to him. There's also uncertainty, because I didn't think it would be this way. I didn't think Sarah and me being together could ever be anything but perfect. And there's the smallest sliver of something that doesn't make any sense for me to feel, a pinprick of light in the darkness. Something that feels—oddly—like hope, although I don't exactly know what I'm hoping for. The truth, I guess, or maybe just clarity—because I don't get it. Why would the whole world change to give me the girl I wished for if nothing is easy when we're together? If there's a part of her that's still in love with her Jeremy? If there's a part of me that's starting to see past my unhealthy obsession of a girl who, maybe, was ever only meant to be a friend, and starting to see the world around me as it really should be?

Sarah puts her hands against her face. "I don't know what's wrong with me. I'm so confused."

I know what's wrong. A boy who was supposed to be her friend ruined her life because he was too selfish to think of anyone but himself.

I wrap my arms around her. "It's okay."

"No, it's not. You deserve so much better than this."

I glance over her shoulder and catch Piper's gaze. I don't know when she ran out of the gym or how much she's heard.

"No," I say, rubbing Sarah's back. "I really don't."

Her tears soak through my shirt.

"Come on," I murmur. "Let's get you home."

She lets me help her up and lead her toward the coat rack, her gaze finding Jeremy briefly before laying her head on my shoulder.

"Jer," I say, overly conscious of how hard Sarah's trying not to look at him. "Could you make sure Piper gets home safely?"

He nods.

"Thanks."

"Graham," he bursts out, "I'm sorry. I don't expect you to forgive me—"

"Don't worry about it."

"But you're my best friend."

"Trust me," I say. "I know how hard it is to not love this girl."

I hear the clicking of heels behind me and glance back just as Piper disappears into the gym. Something deep inside me starts to ache, but not for Sarah. For a life I could have had, if I hadn't messed it up wishing for something else.

✳ ✳ ✳

I call my dad to pick us up. Sarah doesn't speak to me the whole car ride home. She just holds her crown in her hands, slowly turning it, the glow from the exterior Christmas lights bouncing off the manufactured silver and fake gemstones.

Dad parks on the curb next to Sarah's front gate.

"Dad," I say, my throat tight. "Can you give us a minute?"

He nods and gets out of the car, the door creaking open and thudding closed.

Silence stretches between us. I watch the snowflakes drift lazily onto the front windshield. They melt from the heating vents and slide down like rain. "So . . . you and Jeremy?"

She doesn't answer.

"How long has that been going on?"

A single tear trails her cheek as she stares down at her crown. She hesitates.

Then, "I remember the first time Dad took me to the

Christmas Eve parade here in town," she says, her voice distant. "I remember seeing the Christmas queen surrounded
by her court. She looked like a snow princess. The only thing
I'd wanted to be more than her that night was the ballerina
who played Clara in front of city hall. When I told my dad
that, he looked at me and said, 'There's no reason you can't
be both.'" She squeezes her eyes shut tight, tears breaking
through her lashes. "For the longest time, I knew exactly
what I wanted to be—the first girl to be both the Christmas
queen and Clara, and tonight, I got it." She finally meets
my gaze, her watery eyes gleaming. "And it feels worthless."

"Sarah." There's a golf-ball sized lump in my throat and
my mouth feels too dry, and I swear I've never felt my heart
race this fast before. "Are you in love with Jeremy?"

She hesitates. "I don't know."

"Are you in love with me?"

"It feels like I should say yes, but whenever I *really* think
about it, everything is so . . . cloudy. Like there's an answer
hidden in this deep fog that I can't reach. Like there's something I'm supposed to know, but it keeps slipping through
my fingers. I don't know who I want to be with. I don't know
what I want to do with my life. Everything's one giant question mark, and it's terrifying. The one thing I know is that I
need you, Graham. You're the only anchor I have. Without
you, I'm completely lost."

I don't know what to say. I don't know how to tell her that
in another life, she hadn't needed an anchor. She'd known
exactly what she'd wanted, and Jeremy had been a big part
of that picture, but he'd never influenced any of her deci-
sions. She'd wanted to go to a local college and teach ballet
here in Christmas even before she'd started dating him.

How had I forgotten that? She'd talked about it as early
as third grade. Jeremy had supported that dream, but he'd
have supported any dream she'd had. If anything, Sarah had

been Jeremy's anchor. He would've moved anywhere she wanted to go. But here, in this reality, I was trying to change her. I was trying to get her to move to New York because that's where *I* wanted to be. I wanted to drag Sarah into the vision I had for my life instead of shaping a life with her, and nothing about that feels right. Because if you love someone, you should be a team, like my parents are. You should want to shape your lives together. So, either I'm the biggest jerk in the world or—

Or I don't really love Sarah the way I thought I did, and it took screwing up everything for me to finally realize it.

"Sarah. I'm so sorry."

"Why are you apologizing? I should be the one groveling at your feet for being such a horrible girlfriend."

"Never apologize for being honest." I take a deep breath and glance out the window at her house, where her dad is no doubt still up, waiting for his princess to come home. And then suddenly that hits me too, the reason her dad doesn't like me when he used to love Jeremy. Jeremy brought out the best in her. She shined like a literal star, so bright that everyone could see how good they were together. With me, she's . . . dimmer. Confused. Insecure. I don't bring out the best in her.

I bring out the worst.

"Sarah—" I can already hear the defeat in my voice, the reluctant acceptance that we were never meant to be, and Sarah must hear it too because she stops me before I can say anything else.

"Don't," she says. "Not tonight."

"Why?"

"Because my life's too scary without you in it."

I want to tell her I'm not going anywhere. That we were friends before and we'll be friends after. That I'll always be there for her, even though I know that with

Jeremy, she won't need me the way she thinks she does. But I don't know anything about this new world my wish created. I don't know if she can just slide back into being Jeremy's girlfriend without some major repercussions. I don't know if anything can actually go back the way it was or if everything in this reality will always be tainted by my selfishness.

I open my mouth to say something—anything—but the moment passes, and she's pressing her lips against mine, her tears wet on my cheek.

"I'm sure things will be better in the morning," she murmurs.

"Yeah," I say. "Sure."

I get out of the car and open Sarah's door. The snow is two inches thick on the grass already and rising, and Sarah's wearing high heels. She starts to put her feet down, but I stop her.

"Come on," I say, putting my arms around her. "I'll carry you."

She swallows. "You're too good for me, Graham Wallace."

"Trust me, Sarah," I say, lifting her out of the car. "It's definitely the other way around."

I carry her up the front walk to her house. The curtain around the living room window flutters closed, and I know her dad was watching us. He's probably going to have a lot of questions when he sees Sarah's been crying.

If he didn't hate me before, he'll definitely hate me now. I don't put Sarah down until we're underneath her porch awning, where only a dusting of snow frosts the concrete. She smiles up at me, her eyes red and her lips swollen from crying. She places her hand against my cheek.

"Just promise me something," she says.

My own eyes start to burn. "Anything."

"I just . . . I need a little time to think. Can you give me that before you decide where we stand?"

I clear my throat. "I'll give you as much time as you need, so long as you promise me something in return."

"Anything."

"Promise me that you'll put everything aside. Me, Jeremy, your parents' wishes—*everything*—and figure out what will make you happy. You only get one life, Sarah. Don't waste it trying to live up to everyone else's ideas of who you should be."

"Okay. I promise."

She leans forward and kisses my cheek, then opens the door and heads inside. I can hear the faint sounds of *It's a Wonderful Life* playing on the Clarke's TV and Mr. Clarke saying, "Sarah, what's wrong?" just before she shuts the door.

I shove my hands into my pockets as I start down the front path. The snow is seeping through my shoes and into my socks, but I barely feel it. I glance up at the sky, even though I know I won't be seeing any shooting stars tonight. The clouds are too thick, and besides, how many of those does a person actually see in their lifetime?

"God," I whisper into the stillness, "take it back. If she's not meant to be with me, take it back."

I shut my eyes tight, expecting the world to start spinning. Expecting to wake up in my bed on that morning two weeks ago, with everything back the way it was. But when I open my eyes, I'm still standing at Sarah's front gate, my socks drenched, the cold wind biting my cheeks. And Sarah, Jeremy, and Piper are all still miserable.

Because of me.

Mom's waiting when I come in. Dad must have told her something seemed off between Sarah and me. She hears the front door close and pushes up off the couch, turning toward the entry. "How was it?" she asks.

"Fine. I'm going to bed."

"Graham—"

I don't let her see me. She's the one person I couldn't lie to right now, and telling the truth would be impossible. I bound up the stairs and into my room, locking the door behind me. I don't turn on the lights. I don't change out of my suit. I don't answer when Mom knocks. I just lie there on my bed, thinking about how I fell in love with an idealized version of the girl next door, and how it kept me from seeing the girl who'd actually been right for me all along.

✻ ✻ ✻

"Graham—"

14

***

Mom and Dad are sitting at the kitchen table when I come down for breakfast the next morning. Mom's made her signature "cheer up Graham" breakfast—lemon blueberry pancakes doused in warm maple syrup, with fresh strawberries and whipped cream piled on top. There's bacon too, because no one can be properly cheered up without bacon, and a fresh pot of coffee percolating.

"Hi, sweetie," Mom says, getting up from the table. "Coffee?"

Which is how I know she's *really* concerned. My mother would never offer me a coffee in a million years.

But this morning, not only is she pouring me a cup, she's adding peppermint creamer to it. I take the mug from her, murmuring my thanks before sitting in my usual seat and digging into my pancakes. Neither Mom nor Dad says a word, but I can feel their eyes on me.

Finally, Mom asks, "Graham?"

I don't answer her.

"Did something . . . happen . . . between you and Sarah last night?"

"Martha—" Dad starts, as if she shouldn't bring it up, but she ignores him.

"Did you have a fight?"

I shrug. "Not really."

I can hear the frown in her voice. "Did you break up?"

"No. At least, I don't think so."

"Well, what happened?"

"We're just figuring some things out."

Mom opens her mouth, but I stand before she can ask anything else. "I've got to go."

Dad glances at me over his paper. "Go where? We've got church in twenty minutes."

"Piper and I have to finish up the float. I texted her this morning and told her I'd pick her up at eight."

Of course, she hasn't responded, so I have no idea if she slept through it or if she got it and she's ignoring me, but neither of my parents need to know that, and either way, I've got to get out of here.

"Can I take the car?" I ask Dad.

"You can take my car," Mom says. "I don't need it. And here." She gets up and grabs a Ziploc bag of Christmas cookies from the counter. "For sustenance."

I thank her, take the bag, and head for the front door. I don't let myself look at the pictures on the entryway table. It'll only confuse me more, seeing images of the life I always wanted when I'm starting to think it was never mine to have.

✳✳✳

Piper barely says two words to me when I pick her up. I try to bring up last night while we work, but every time I do, Piper says, "We've only got six more hours until the parade.

We need to concentrate." Or, "Did you finish cutting out those snowflakes yet?" Or, "Where are the scissors?"

She's all business, and I go along with it, partly because we really do need to finish the float, and partly because I have no idea where to start anyway.

Piper, I know how last night looked, but I can explain. You see, we're actually in an alternate universe. I used to think I was in love with Sarah Clarke, but then I made this wish on a shooting star and she became my girlfriend, but she's really supposed to be Jeremy's girlfriend, and it took everything in my life changing for me to realize I'm really supposed to be with you.

Yeah. I don't think so.

"Well, whether it's done or not," Piper says, dusting off her hands, "we've run out of time."

I glance up from a snowflake I'm pretty sure I've spent the last hour hanging. "Huh?"

She holds up her phone. 4:00 p.m. One hour until the parade.

I shake my head. "Yikes, yeah. Mr. Campbell's going to be here with the truck any minute."

"And I've got to get back home if I'm going to change into my uniform in time."

"Okay, yeah. Let's go."

I jump down off the float and take a few steps back to give it one last look.

Paper snowflakes dangle from invisible wires while swirls of white cotton cover the top of the flatbed. Christmas lights wrap around book trees, carefully woven around the titles, all of which are written in big reflective lettering so they can be seen in the dark. In the middle of it all, a giant scroll reads, *Books Open Doors to Worlds Unexplored*, and on either side of the skirt, the words *Merry Christmas from Aunt Bee's Bookstore* are written in alternating red-and-green letters.

"It's incredible," I say, taking it all in.

"Not bad for eight days' work," Piper agrees, standing beside me. "We make a good team."

I glance at her.

She looks at me.

"Piper—"

"Whatever you're going to say, I don't want to hear it."

She starts toward the car, her arms crossed, her head tucked down.

"But you don't understand." The words tumble out of my mouth as I follow her, my heart suddenly beating so hard at the sight of her turning her back on me, of wanting nothing to do with me, I can feel it in my throat. "If you'd just let me explain—"

Piper whirls around. Her eyes are shiny with tears, but she doesn't look sad.

She looks furious.

I take a step back.

"You made me feel like an idiot last night, Graham."

"I know, and I'm—"

"What? Sorry? What exactly are you sorry for? Leading me on? Acting like you like me, like you *care*? Almost kissing me not once but *twice*, and both times pulling away to go be with her? Or maybe you feel sorry for making me think *I* was the one who crossed a line that night we danced in here, that I was some pathetic girl throwing herself at a guy who was already taken, when you were really the one who was crossing lines left and right and not even caring who it hurt?"

"That's just it. It's taken me a while to realize it, but—"

"And I get it," she continues, ignoring me, "I'm not a total moron. Sarah is your girlfriend, and from the looks of things, she and your best friend have feelings for each other.

So I get why you had to deal with that last night, but when you held her and you told Jeremy you know how hard it is not to love her—that's when I knew. Sarah's the one for you. It's always going to be her."

"Piper, if you'd just let me explain—"

"I don't need to *let* you do anything because even if Sarah's not the one for you, the way you've led me on is bullshit, Graham, and you know it. So, no. I don't want to hear your explanations. I don't want to get caught up in whatever sick game you're playing. I don't want *anything* from you, except for you to take me home."

"But—"

"I'm telling you, Graham. One more word from you, and I'll scream."

I can't help it. The thought makes me smile. "Promise?"

She takes a deep breath.

"Okay, okay." I hold up my hands. "I won't say another word. Well, maybe one."

She glares at me.

"I'm sorry," I say. "The last thing I would ever want is for you to feel like I've been stringing you along. I know what that feels like, and it sucks."

"That's more than one word," she says.

"Yeah, it is. But I had to say it."

Headlights flash as Mr. Campbell edges his truck up to the barn. He sticks his head out the driver's side window.

"All set?" he asks.

I nod.

He puts his truck in reverse and turns around so he can back up to the float.

"Go ahead and get in the car," I tell Piper, handing her Mom's keys. "I'll help him hitch it up."

She takes the keys and starts for the car, then stops and turns back to me.

"I don't just *feel* like you've been stringing me along, Graham," she says, softly. "I know you have."

And just when I thought I couldn't feel any lower, that sinks me, because it's true. I didn't mean to do it. I was just as confused by everything as she was. But I treated her just like Sarah treated me, and—

And suddenly, I get it. I don't think the Sarah in my previous life ever felt the same way for me that I've been feeling for Piper, but just like I didn't mean to string Piper along, I don't think Sarah meant to string me along either. Even if she got some enjoyment out of knowing I liked her, I don't think she ever flirted with me vindictively. I think there are too many levels to a person and the reasons why they do things to give such a surface-level judgment on anything. If Piper could have read my thoughts all the times we've been together, she would've known why I kept stopping myself short from kissing her. Why I kept getting close only to push her away.

Why I've felt so guilty for falling in love with her.

Because that's what happened. I've tried to deny it. God knows it probably makes me the worst sort of person, to wish for one girl and fall for another, but I couldn't stop it any more than the earth can stop circling the sun. It was an inevitable, unchangeable force.

I only regret that I didn't realize all of this before making that stupid wish. Now, I don't know if things *can* go back to the way they were. Which means I'm going to need to make things right. With Sarah, with Jeremy, and definitely with Piper. But she clearly isn't open to hearing anything I have to say at the moment, and I need to finally end things with Sarah before I try to explain myself to Piper anyway.

I need to fix what I've broken if any of us are going to have a chance at true happiness.

✱✱✱

Piper and I are silent during ride back to her house. I drop her off and say, "See you at the parade," but she doesn't answer me. I wait until she's safely inside, then head for the bookstore.

Aunt Bee's shrugging into her coat when I walk in.

"Oh good, Graham. Be a dear and flip that sign, will you?" she asks, wrapping her scarf around her neck. "Going to join me on the float?"

"I don't think so," I say, flipping the sign on the front door to *CLOSED* and locking it. "I'm not really good at having people gawk at me."

"Oh, and I am?"

"Bee, you were born for it."

She laughs and swats my arm.

"Besides," I say, following her to the back door, "I want to see Sarah dance."

"Ah. Boyfriend duties?"

"Something like that." We step out into the back alley, then start for Second Street, where the floats are idling, waiting for the parade to begin. "Can I walk you to the float?"

"Aren't you sweet? But see"—she gestures to the mouth of the alley, where Mr. Campbell is bouncing on the balls of his feet and breathing into his cupped hands—"Bill's waiting for me."

My brow furrows. "Aunt Bee, can I ask you a question?"

"Sure thing." She checks her watch. "We've still got five minutes."

"It's sort of personal."

"Those are my favorite kind."

I shouldn't ask—it's definitely one of those questions my mom would call intrusive—but I have to know.

"Why did you and Mr. Campbell break up?"

She sighs, but she doesn't look offended by the question.

"Divorce, Graham," she says quietly, her gaze drifting back to Mr. Campbell. "When the two people in question are married, it's called divorce." Her eyes go a little hazy, like she's seeing something else, something beyond this alley and this town and this moment. "We got married young, which isn't a guarantee for divorce, mind—most couples we know got married young and have been together ever since—but we tied the knot before we realized that the love we shared wasn't the kind of love you get married on. We grew apart instead of growing together, and before we knew it, we were bringing out the worst in each other. Maybe we could have made it work if we weren't both so stubborn and set in our ways, but it would've meant a lot of compromising of who we were at the core of ourselves, and neither one of us wanted to do that."

She looks back at me.

"Choosing who to spend your life with is serious business, Graham. It's not just about loving someone—people fall in and out of love every day. It's about building your life with someone. You want that person to bring out the best version of you, and you want to do the same for them. That doesn't mean it won't take some work—loving someone for the rest of your life is a choice you make every day—but when it's all said and done, you have to complement each other on the most foundational of levels."

"Yeah, I'm starting to get that."

"Bill and I—we realized we were better off friends than we were partners. I wish it wasn't true. Marriage should be for the long haul. But for us, we just couldn't make it work, so we decided to get out before we did any more damage to each other."

Aunt Bee must see something in my expression because she knocks her thumb against the underside of my chin.

"If something's not right," she says, gently, "it's better to realize it now, before it's too late."

"Thanks, Aunt Bee."

She winks. "Anytime, kid."

I watch her walk down the alley. Mr. Campbell waits for her with a big smile. For a second, I think he might put his arm around her, but he keeps his hands in his pockets and nods at something she says. They walk off together, side by side, shoulders close but not quite touching, content with the distance between them. I can't help but wonder: Did they fall in love with an idealized version of each other instead of the real thing? Did they darken each other's light, the way I've been darkening Sarah's?

If I've learned anything, it's that love's a much more complicated thing than I ever thought it could be, and yet, on that foundational level Aunt Bee was talking about, it's very simple.

Sarah was never meant to be mine, and I was never meant to be hers.

15

I stand behind a group of kids in front of city hall holding empty bags, waiting to collect the candies and dollar toys that will soon litter the street. The parade begins with our high school band playing "Joy to the World", and I spot Piper in the group of cheerleaders that follow, all dressed up in their red-and-white track suits and Santa hats, shaking their pom-poms and doing cartwheels and back handsprings. Piper's doing a good job of smiling and cheering, a total pro, but there's a slight downturn to her lips in between the smiles, a tiny furrowing of her brow. It's not enough for anyone else to pick up on, but I've been studying Piper's expressions for weeks—maybe even longer than I realized—and I can see the anger and betrayal hidden underneath.

I want to follow her as she continues down the street, but I force myself to stay put.

One thing at a time.

The Christmas king and queen don't make their appearance until the end, when they ride in on the float just before Santa's sleigh, so the ballet performance will come first. I rub my hands and blow hot air onto them to keep warm. In front of me, city councilors dressed as elves throw chocolate bars to the kids. A little girl wearing braids and a gap-toothed smile glances back at me.

"Want one?" she asks.

"Sure," I say, taking the Milky Way she offers. "Thanks."

I start to tear open the wrapper, then realize she's still staring at me.

"What's up?" I ask.

"Everything will be okay," she says. "You'll see."

"What? How do you—?"

She turns back to the parade, a knowing smile on her face.

I throw the candy in her bag when she's not looking.

"Ladies and gentlemen," an announcer says into a microphone behind me, "the Christmas Ballet Academy proudly presents: *The Nutcracker.*"

I've seen this same sequence every year since I can remember. It begins with all of the ballerinas dancing in a tight circle that slowly unfolds to reveal Clara in the middle. Sarah has played Clara for the past four years, and apparently my brain is so used to seeing her in that role that it takes me a second to realize the girl who steps out when the circle opens isn't Sarah.

My brow furrows and my gaze darts from ballerina to ballerina, looking for her, but she's not there. I take my phone out of my pocket and text her.

Where are you?

Three dots appear.

In the alley behind city hall, she replies.

I text back: Stay there.

I make my way through the crowd, then dart around

the concession booths and into the alley. She's sitting on the back steps of city hall, the music of the parade and the sounds of chattering voices from the next street over filling the space around her. Her hair is up in her ballerina bun, and I can see the tulle of her Clara costume peeking out from beneath her coat.

I kneel in front of her. "What's going on? Are you okay?"

She shakes her head. "I just suddenly realized . . . I don't want it. I don't want Juilliard. I love to dance, but trying to make a career out of it is killing me. I hate the protein shakes and the extra practices. My feet are covered in blisters and my toenails are shredding off and my hair's falling out from the stress of it all, and I'm sorry," she sobs, tears breaking free from her lashes and rolling down her cheeks. "I'm so sorry, but I just don't want the future you want. I thought I did, but—"

"Hey." I wrap my arms around her and pull her against me. "It's okay."

She lays her head on my shoulder. "It's not okay because I don't know what I want, and I'm scared, Graham. I'm so scared."

"There's nothing to be scared of. You're sixteen. No one knows what they want at sixteen."

"My parents did."

"Yeah, well, your parents are freaks."

She laughs.

"And besides," I say. "I know what you want to do. What you always said you wanted to do anyway."

"Oh yeah?" she asks. "What's that?"

I pull away from her, just enough to meet her gaze. "You want to open up a dance studio here in Christmas. You want to get married and raise a family here and stay close to your own family. You never wanted a big city life until I mentioned it. You never wanted Juilliard until I put the idea in your head. You want to be a businesswoman—a damn good one at that—and you want to teach little girls and boys to love dance the way that you do. And—"

I hesitate. Because even though I know it's the right thing—for her, for me, for everybody—something lurches inside my stomach at the realization that I'm finally giving it up: the made-up version of Sarah I fell in love with; the idea that she and I were supposed to be together, when clearly it was never meant to be; and all of those sleepless nights, wishing she were mine. Two entire years of my life spent with an aching heart, wanting something that was never mine to have, all leading up to this moment.

Sarah Clarke has been haunting me for too long. This is the night I set her free.

"And you want to be with Jeremy."

She frowns. "Graham—"

"No, it's okay. *I'm* okay. You two belong together."

"But I love *you*."

"You love an idea of me. Something planted in your head that was never supposed to be there."

She shakes her head. "I don't understand."

"Trust me. You need to be with Jeremy. I think everything will become clear if you just go find him."

"Are you breaking up with me?"

"Sarah, I wish you knew how ridiculous I sound to myself right now. You're my dream girl. I always thought that if you were mine, I'd make you happy. But I don't. You're miserable with me. You should be out there dancing, and instead you're sitting in an alley, crying your eyes out, not sure of yourself or what you're doing with your life, and it's all because of me. I'm not breaking up with you. I'm giving you your life back."

Her tears come faster now, and her voice is so small, I have to strain to hear it. "What if I don't want it back?"

"You're only saying that because you don't know the real you. I took that away from you. Now I need you to go out there and find it again."

"By being with Jeremy?"

"No. Jeremy doesn't make you who you are. He just knows how to lift you up so you can shine." I place my hands on either side of her face, brushing her tears away with my thumbs, and then lean my forehead against hers, my own eyes prickling. "I'm so sorry I did this to you."

"I'm sorry too," she says, her hands braceleting my wrists. "I really wanted this to work."

I laugh, a strangled sound. "Me too."

She gives my wrists one last squeeze. "We'll still be friends, right? No matter what?"

"Always," I promise. "Now go find Jeremy. I'm telling you, you guys are like the other half of each other. I think that fog you've been feeling will lift the second you're with him."

She nods and pushes off the stoop. She starts down the steps, then stops and turns back to me. "I really don't know what I'd do without you, Graham."

"I feel the same way about you."

"So, our Friday morning doughnut tradition . . . ?"

"Still on. I honestly don't know how I'd survive without it."

"Me neither." She smiles, and I think it might be the first truly authentic spark of happiness I've seen from her in this fake, twisted world. "Goodbye, Graham."

"Goodbye, Sarah."

She turns and pulls out her phone. She hits a button, then holds it to her ear. I hear her say, "Jeremy? Where are you?" as she walks away, back toward the parade.

And deep inside, something starts to break.

I glance up at the sky, but the stars are covered by thick low-hanging clouds. No chance of seeing a shooting star tonight, and really, I have no clue if wishing on one would even work a second time. I thread my fingers behind my head and breathe deep to stave off the rising surge of panic.

My gaze snags on a church across the street. First Presbyterian. It's not ours—we go to the nondenominational church on Front Street—and I know logically that God can hear me standing in front of this stoop just as clearly as He can hear me in a church, Creator of the universe and all, but there's a tug in my chest, a need to be somewhere hushed and sacred.

I cross the street and head for the darkened church. My hand grips the doorknob, and my first prayer is that the door will open. My thumb presses down on the latch, and the door slips forward from the frame. I glance over my shoulder, but there's no one on the street. Still, I don't want anyone to think I'm trespassing, so I call out, "Hello?" as I step inside.

No answer.

The carpeted floor creaks as I move down the aisle and slip into a pew. There's a nativity scene on the altar and a large wooden cross hanging on the wall behind it. Songbooks and bibles line the little shelf that runs the length of the pew in front of me. I think of this game I played when I was a kid, when I would pray on something really hard—usually a new gaming system or a passing grade on a test I didn't study for—and then open up the bible to a random page and use it like a magic-eight ball. Sometimes it worked and I got something that seemed like an answer. Sometimes I opened it to a page with a bunch of complicated names begetting other names, which I always took as God's way of saying, "Ask again later."

I almost do it now out of habit, but I haven't come looking for an answer—I've come looking to make things right. I clasp my hands in my lap and stare at the nativity, my eyes resting on the baby sleeping in the manger.

"God," I whisper into the quiet, "I really messed things

up this time. I never would've made that wish if I'd known it would come true." I hesitate. "Okay, that's a lie. When I made that wish, I would've done anything to be with Sarah. I didn't understand that just because you think you're supposed to be with someone doesn't mean you actually are."

An image of Piper pops into my head, smiling at me and tossing her hair to the side as she laughed at a joke I had made.

My throat tightens.

"I didn't know that I could get so blinded by what I thought was right only to miss what was right in front of me."

My eyes burn. I blink back the tears and take a deep breath.

"I get it now. I get what You were trying to show me. I mean, that's the reason You let all of this happen, right? So I would learn my lesson? Well, I've learned it. So, please, put it back. Put the world back to the way it should be, before I messed everything up."

I close my eyes and count to three, but when I open them again, I'm still sitting in the pew, and from what I can tell, nothing's changed. So I close them again, tighter, and wait a minute. Then two minutes.

Then five.

I start to get frustrated, but then I remember that the wish didn't happen right away. The world only changed after I went to sleep.

"Okay, God," I say. "You win. I'll go home."

And then, because I can't help myself, I grab the nearest bible and randomly open to a page in Ecclesiastes. My gaze lands on a verse:

This also is vanity and grasping for the wind.

Well, that's reassuring.

I put the bible back and stand.

"Please," I whisper one more time.

Then I turn and start for home.

16

✱✱✱

I wake at seven in the morning to the sound of bacon frying in a pan and Frank Sinatra singing "Have Yourself a Merry Little Christmas", darkness still pressing against the window.

I pull the pillow over my head, intending to go back to sleep, but everything comes back to me in a flash. The dance—pulling Piper close, Sarah running away. The parade—Sarah telling me she didn't want the life we had planned together, and me sending her back to Jeremy. The church—feeling my whole world crashing down around me and begging God to put everything back to normal.

I jump out of bed and into the hall, shooting past Dad who comes up short outside his bedroom door, muttering, "Well, good morning and a merry Christmas to you too."

My feet hammer down the stairs as I practically throw myself at the entryway table, scooping up every picture, rifling through them one by one.

Me and Sarah.

Me and Sarah.

Me and Sarah.

Nothing's changed. I've still been with Sarah the past two years. She's still wasted her time and happiness on someone who was never right for her. And Piper—

Whatever I could've had in my old life with Piper, whatever purity there might have been in our relationship, is gone. Now I can only hope to salvage something real and good between us out of the wreckage I've caused.

Maybe it'll be fine. Maybe we can all find some way to get back on track here. I'm the only one who knows anything is wrong anyway, that we're all living shadow lives of what we were meant to live.

Still, I won't pretend my heart doesn't shatter, my faith disappearing completely, as I glance up at the ceiling and whisper, "Why didn't You change it?"

"Why didn't who change what?" Dad asks groggily, running his hand over the back of his head and yawning as he comes to a stop behind me.

"Nothing," I mutter as the kitchen phone—our only landline—rings. I head into the family room and plop down onto the couch, staring at the Christmas tree and the presents wrapped in shiny paper underneath.

"Hello?" Mom's voice echoes from the kitchen as she answers the phone. "Mary Lou? What's wrong? What do you mean you haven't seen her?"

Piper.

I jump up from the couch and bolt into the kitchen. "Mom?"

She glances at me, her brows drawing together as she speaks into the phone. "Did she come home from the parade last night?"

I press my ear against the receiver.

"Yes, yes," I hear Queenie say. "She came home last night

and went to bed, but when I went in to wake her up for breakfast, she wasn't there. Now, I'm sure she's fine"—a half sob punctures the line—"but would your boy happen to know where she is?"

Mom pulls her head back to look at me.

I take the phone from her.

"Queenie? It's Graham."

"Oh, Graham. Thank goodness. I'm just—I'm worried. It isn't like her to leave so early without telling me, and I can't imagine where she'd go on Christmas day—"

"Queenie," I say interrupting her, "did anything happen last night?" I think of Jordan, and my jaw tightens. "Did a boy come over?"

"Heavens, no. Piper knows better than that. Besides, she hasn't brought any boys to the house other than you," she replies. "Her father called after the parade to tell her he wouldn't be able to make it for Christmas after all and I could tell she was upset even though she told him she understood, but you don't think that's why she's missing, do you?"

I think of the look on Piper's face every time she talks about the divorce, the way she tries to cover up the fact that her heart is breaking and no one else seems to care.

We had one Christmas tradition my parents never broke, no matter how busy they were.

Oh God.

"Queenie, I think I know where she is, and if I'm right, she might be hurt, so I need you to do something for me, okay? Call 9-1-1 and ask for an ambulance to go to Mr. Turlington's pond, understand? You know where that is, don't you?"

"Yes, I—"

I thrust the phone at Mom. "Make sure an ambulance gets there."

"Graham," Mom sputters.

But I'm already in the entryway, stuffing Dad's keys in my pocket, throwing on a pair of boots, and sprinting out the door. There's an inch of snow on the windshield, but it's already starting to melt from the warmer-than-normal temperature and it wipes off on my sleeve. I jump into the car, start the engine, put it in reverse, and then I'm gone, going forty on a twenty-five, my heart pounding in my chest as I rev it up to forty-five. I want to go faster, but the sun is only just starting to rise and I won't have much reaction time if a kid or a deer jumps in front of my car.

"Please be okay." I say it over and over again. "Please be okay, please be okay, please—"

I push it to sixty-five on the country road, praying no cops are out to pull me over. Even if they were, I wouldn't stop. I couldn't, knowing the ice is too thin, and if Piper decided to skate—

There's a road that leads to Turlington's house and then the pond next to it, but the pond is just here, on the other side of these trees, so I swerve off the interstate and park in the grass. I don't even know if I grab the keys or close the door behind me. All I can think is, *Piper.*

I sprint through the trees, cold air biting my skin. For the first time I realize I never grabbed a coat and I'm out here in only a T-shirt, flannel pajama pants, and Dad's work boots. I can hear sirens in the distance, but they're still too far away, when minutes can mean the difference between life and death. I break through the trees, my eyes searching for any sign of her.

Everything stops.

I see her shoes on the bench. Skate marks on the ice.

And the hole that's opened up in the middle of the pond.

Everything in me shuts down. I think I shout her name as I race to the edge of the pond where she went in. I think I throw my shoes off to lighten my weight because there's a stinging in the bottom of my feet as I race across the ice. All I know for sure is Piper is in that water and the sirens are coming but they won't get here in time. *I* might not even be here in time, but I have to try.

I take a deep breath and jump.

The water is like a thousand knives stabbing me all at once. I suck in a breath and my lungs fill with water. Everything in me tells me to swim up, to get out, to get *air*, but I push myself down, into the reeds. My eyes burn, and I can barely see anything in the dawn glow just beginning to filter through the ice. Everything is shadows and billowing shapes around me. I reach my hands through the algae, but there's nothing. My lungs are screaming at me now. I have to go up. I need to breathe.

And then—

I feel a hand against mine. Lifeless and only slightly warmer than the water surrounding it. I grab it and pull, but her body doesn't move. I swim down farther, finding the place where her skate is caught in the weeds. I pull it off her foot, and her body comes free. I wrap my arms around her torso and kick up, toward the light.

We break the surface, and air fights the water in my chest, pushing it out in hacking coughs. I try to lift Piper onto the ice, but my limbs are numb and every last ounce of strength has left my body.

The sirens are loud now. I can see their flashing through the trees.

"Over here!" I shout, squeezing Piper tighter against me, willing any body heat I have left to transfer to her. "Quick!"

I push her hair out of her face and hug her close, my body shaking as the ice seeps into my veins.

The paramedics break through the trees, carrying a stretcher between them. I hear them shout something at us, but the world's getting dimmer, and their voices are stretching into sounds I don't understand.

"I'm here, Piper. You're going to be okay," I murmur into her ear, my teeth chattering on every syllable, but she doesn't respond. She's not breathing, and there's no pulse in her neck.

I hold her tighter.

"It's okay. People are here now. You're going to be okay."

And then they tear her body away from mine and pull us both out of the water.

17

✳✳✳

The hospital smells like disinfectant and stale coffee.

I haven't seen Piper since they split us up in the emergency room, taking us each to different beds and flinging the curtains around us. I could hear the flurry of people moving around her, saying things like, "paddles" and "ventilator" and "life support". I kept trying to tell them that she was fine, that things weren't supposed to be this way, and that the real Piper was back in another time and she was never supposed to be here, in this hospital, so they didn't need to worry about her, she was fine, but then they shoved something into my IV, and everything went dark.

Mom and Dad got here first. They brought Piper's grandma with them—I was just lucid enough to see her race to Piper's bed and hear the doctors tell her they were moving Piper to another room. I wanted to tell them they didn't need to do that, that none of this was real—it *couldn't* be real—but I couldn't make a sound.

"It's okay, honey," Mom said. "We're here."

I tried to tell her with my eyes—tried to let her know that I screwed up and I needed her or the doctors or someone to fix it. That I needed Piper to be okay. That I needed her to be back in the bookstore, pulling books from the shelf and biting her lip and trying to decide which one to get. That I needed her to be back in that barn, making that parade float, only this time Sarah and I wouldn't be together, and I'd be free to feel all the things for Piper I've been feeling, all the things I told myself I couldn't feel because the whole world changed for me to be with Sarah, because I made a stupid wish and now everything had gone wrong.

But Mom didn't see any of it. She was talking to the doctor. He was telling her I was going to be okay, that my core body temperature was almost back to normal. I'd be groggy from the sedative they gave me but I'd be coming out of it soon, and he was right. The world was sharpening around me, but my tongue still wouldn't move, and no one gave a damn that none of it was real, none of it was actually happening, that it couldn't be, it couldn't, *it couldn't*.

"And the girl?" Dad asked. "Piper?"

"We can only legally tell her parents and emergency contacts how she's doing." The doctor took a deep breath. "But we're doing everything we can."

It was another hour before the effects of the drug wore off enough for me to speak. I stopped talking about the Piper who was safe in another time when I noticed the doctor looking at me like I needed a psych evaluation. It was another three hours before they felt good enough to discharge me and another two hours after that before we were cleared to go home.

But we didn't go home. I wouldn't let Mom and Dad take me.

"Graham, I talked to Mary Lou," Mom said. "Her dad

is here now, and her mom is on the way. There's nothing we can do."

I glared at her. "You two can go home. I'm staying."

"You need to get some rest," Mom started to say, but Dad put a hand on her arm.

"Of course we're staying," he said. "Of course."

I changed into the dry clothes Mom brought from home, and we headed to the third floor, where they had taken Piper. The nurse was kind enough to tuck an electric blanket around me.

The chill is still intense, even though my temp is in a safe range, and now Dad's on his third coffee, I'm on my second, and Mom is scrolling through her phone, reading off random facts about hypothermia she keeps finding on the internet. My heart jumps every time the door opens and someone either enters or exits Piper's room. Doctors and nurses and technicians. In and out. In and out.

I keep looking for some sign from them that she's getting better, that she's going to be okay, but they don't even look at us, and I don't know if it's because they're so busy, or because they know if they did, they'd give her condition away, and the weight of it would be too much for us to bear.

The door opens again, and Piper's dad steps out. His eyes are red and swollen and his hair and clothes are disheveled, like he's done nothing but sob since he got here. My first thought is, *Good.* I want him to suffer. I want him to know this wouldn't have happened if he had just put his daughter first for once in his life. But then I remember he's not responsible.

I did this. Piper wouldn't be here if it wasn't for me.

He grabs his phone and calls someone. I'm guessing Piper's mom. He walks as he talks, and all I hear is, "Where are you now?" before he disappears around a corner.

Queenie comes out next.

"Graham," she says. "You can see her now."

I hand Dad my coffee and stand, leaving my blanket on the chair. I hear Mom ask how Piper is doing, and I hear Queenie say, "They're keeping her going until her mom can get here, but there's nothing more they can do," as I step into the room and close the door behind me.

There's a tube down Piper's throat and a machine hooked up to her, inflating her lungs. There's no color at all left in her skin, and her eyes are sunken-in craters, but her hair is still golden against the white pillowcase beneath her head, and if I look at just that, if I ignore the beeping and the whirring and the tubes and the too-clean scent of medicine and sterilized equipment, I could almost think she was sleeping.

I sit down in the seat next to her and take her hand in mine, remembering the way it felt, warm and strong and alive at the dance, when all I wanted was to be with her.

God, how could You let this happen?

"I'm sorry, Piper." My tears come fast now as I press my forehead against her arm. "I'm so sorry. I should've been there. I should've stopped this. I should've never made that wish. I should've—God, I don't know. I don't know what I could have done." I glance up at the ceiling. "God, please. I was an idiot. Please, make this right."

I stay like that, hunched over her, tears hot against my cheeks, until Piper's dad comes back into the room. He clears his throat like he wants to say something to me, and all I can think is, *Don't you dare thank me for going in after her. I'm the reason she's here.*

But he must sense that too, or he just can't find the words, because he says nothing, and neither do my parents when we drive back home.

A numbness takes over me as I walk past the family room, past the Christmas presents still sitting unopened under the tree. Mom tries to follow me up the staircase, but Dad tells her to let me go.

I don't know what I'm supposed to do.

I lie down on my bed and close my eyes.

I try to stay awake. It feels wrong somehow, to just go to sleep. To do nothing. But my body is done fighting, and when I close my eyes, the last thing I see is Piper standing beneath the glow of the old barn light, disappearing in wisps of smoke.

18

***

I wake to the voice of Gene Autry singing "Here Comes Santa Claus" at six o'clock in the morning. Rage fills me up like battery acid. I fling the covers off of me—covers Mom must have put on because I definitely fell asleep on top of my bed—and fly down the stairs.

"Mom!"

She pokes her head out of the kitchen, a spatula in her hand and her poinsettia apron dusted with flour. "What?"

"What the hell is wrong with you?"

She's so startled, she doesn't even think to reprimand me. "What do you mean?"

"How can you be playing that music? Now, of all days? *How can you not care?*"

"Care about what? Graham, honey, what's gotten into you?"

I'm about to ask her if she has a giant hole where her heart used to be, but then my gaze snags on the entryway table.

The pictures.

They're all back to normal. Awkward sixth-grade me.

Sunburnt on a beach in Mexico me. Fat, wrinkly baby me.

Sarah isn't in any of them.

I turn slowly and look past Mom, into the kitchen, where star-shaped Christmas cookies are cooling on a rack. Where the coffee pot is brewing and the radio switches to Bing Crosby's "I'll Be Home for Christmas".

"Mom," I say, my voice breaking. "What day is it?"

Her brow furrows. "It's the eighth."

"Of December?"

"Yes," she huffs out, her hand on her hip. "What has gotten into you?"

I vault forward. "Mom, have I been dating Sarah Clarke for the past two years?"

Her eyes widen. She turns her head slightly toward the stairs. "Tom? I think your son's having a nervous breakdown."

"Coming," Dad calls.

"Mom, please," I say, "just answer the question."

"No, honey. You haven't been dating Sarah Clarke." She puts her hand on my forehead. "Are you feeling okay? Did you have a bad dream?"

I shake my head. "You can't imagine."

"What's up?" Dad asks, looping his tie around his neck as he starts down the stairs.

I thread my hands through my hair, my mind racing. "Are you sure I've never dated Sarah?"

"Yes, Graham," Mom says. "I'm sure."

"And Jeremy's not a wrestler?"

"That gangly boy?" Dad asks. "He'd get pummeled in two seconds flat."

"And Piper—"

I can't even finish the question.

"Who's Piper?" Mom asks.

Oh my God.

"It worked," I breathe. "I mean, He worked. I mean—" I let out a *whoop* and wrap my mom up in a giant hug, spinning her around. "I've never dated Sarah Clarke! I've never dated Sarah Clarke! *Thank You, God!*"

"I wouldn't yell that around Sarah," Dad mutters. "She might take it the wrong way."

"Graham, put me down," Mom says, smacking my chest. "Are you hallucinating? Is he hallucinating, Tom?"

I set her down and run my hands through my hair. "No, Mom, I'm not hallucinating. I'm— Wait, what time is it?"

Dad checks his watch. "Six-fifteen."

Piper. I have to see Piper.

"I've got to go," I say, grabbing my coat.

"Go where?" Mom asks. "You aren't dressed for school, and you haven't even eaten your breakfast."

"I don't need it." I pull on one shoe, then the other, grabbing Dad's keys from the hook. "But I do need these."

"Hey—" Dad says.

"I'll be back before you need to leave. I just have to check something."

Dad shakes his head, flabbergasted. "Okay."

"Thanks." I start for the door. "Oh, and Mom? Sarah's going to be waiting for me outside in about thirty minutes. Tell her I'm running late and I'll catch up with her at school."

Mom puts her hands on her hips. "Young man, I would like to know what's going on."

"Later," I promise, even though I have no clue what I could possibly say to explain any of this, but I don't care.

I have to see Piper.

I take the fastest route with the least amount of stop signs and get to Queenie's house in three minutes flat. The Christmas lights I put up for her are gone. There's a light on in the living room, so I know someone's up. I ring the doorbell, bouncing on the balls of my feet. I curl my fingers into my palms, gritting my teeth to stop myself from barreling through the door.

Why is it taking so long for them to answer?

I reach for the doorbell again just as the knob turns.

Piper.

She has a pin between her teeth and her hair scooped up in one hand. Her skin is flushed, her eyes are clear, and her breathing is the most beautiful sound I've ever heard.

"Yes?" she asks, expertly weaving a hair tie around her ponytail.

All the breath leaves my body. "Oh, thank God, you're all right."

She pauses, her hands still in her hair. There's only a slight hint of familiarity in her gaze. She takes a strand of hair and wraps it around the tie, sliding the pin through the strand to hold it in place. "Do I know you?"

And then I realize that if I never dated Sarah Clarke—if none of that "other reality" stuff happened and it really is December eighth, then Piper and I have never properly met each other, let alone spent enough time together for me to know that her favorite book is *Little Women*, or that she writes notes in the margins of everything she reads. I'm not supposed to know that she's never bowled before but she's a phenomenal dancer, or that her parents are getting divorced and her favorite memory of her family is skating together every Christmas morning. I'm not supposed to know that special way she laughs when I say something funny, that melodic tinkling sound that stirs an almost spiritual reverence inside of me. I'm not supposed to know how funny she is or how smart or how kind or how brave.

I'm not supposed to know anything about her, other than her name and that she's a cheerleader and that she picks out one book a week from the bookstore.

I take a step back and try to give my eyes a shape that says I haven't been falling in love with her for the past two and a half weeks. I try to stifle my excitement at seeing her alive, breath in her lungs and light in her eyes, and I try to think of some reason why I would be here, on her porch, at the crack of dawn on a school day.

"I, uh, I work at Aunt Bee's bookstore." I clear my throat and take a shot in the dark, hoping that some of the things that happened in the other reality—because it *was* real, wasn't it?—were the same things that were going to happen here, regardless of my wish. "She wanted to know if you're still coming in for training tomorrow?"

Her eyes widen. "Yes, of course! You're the guy who works the register."

I smirk. "Guilty."

"Yeah, I'll be there." Piper leans against the doorframe, her arms crossed. "But why didn't she just call me? And why does she need to know at"—she pulls her phone out of her back pocket and checks the time—"six-thirty in the morning?"

"I was, uh"—I put my hands in my pockets—"I was just on my way to school, so I told her I'd stop by and ask."

"And how do you know where I live, Mystery Boy?"

I shrug. "Everyone knows where Queenie lives."

Good, I think. *Smooth.*

"You call her Queenie too?"

I laugh, a nervous sound. "Doesn't everybody?"

She scrunches up her nose. "I don't think so."

"Sorry, let's start over." I hold out my hand. "I'm Graham. Graham Wallace."

She stares at my hand for a moment, her lips tugging into that half smirk I love so much.

"Piper Hudson," she says, taking my hand. "But I guess you already knew that."

"Yes, I did, but it's still nice to meet you. You know. Officially."

"You too, Graham Wallace."

"So, I . . . guess I'll see you tomorrow?"

She pulls her hand away, and her smile grows. "Not if I see you first."

"Good one." I put my hands in my pockets. "All right. Well. See you."

I start down the walkway, but then I stop and turn back.

"Oh, by the way, we're supposed to get a new shipment of books in tomorrow, so you might have to rethink whatever book you were going to buy next."

"Excuse me?"

"You know, your system? Where you comb through the new arrivals like you're going to pick up something else, but then you just end up buying one of the books you ogled the last time you were there?"

"Ah, so the jig is up."

"Let's be honest," I say, "the jig was never really down to begin with."

Piper's lips part, and she stares at me like she's trying to grasp something tenuous and fading. "Have we had this conversation before?"

Yes.

I shake my head. "I don't think so."

"Sorry, I just have the strangest feeling, like—"

"Déjà vu?"

"Yeah."

"Me too." I take a step back, my eyes locked on hers, and for a moment, I let everything I feel for her shine through them—every conversation we've ever had, every time she made me laugh, every time I wanted to kiss her so badly I thought I might break apart from the sheer force of it. "See you around, Piper Hudson."

Her brow furrows. "See you around, Graham Wallace."

I slide into my car and start for home. I wait until I turn off her street, just in case she's still watching, and then I smack my hands against the steering wheel. "Thank you, thank you, thank you!"

And in a still, small, quiet place in my heart, I suddenly know why my wish came true. It wasn't so that I would learn Sarah Clark and I aren't soulmates (though that was a much-needed lesson).

It was so that Piper could be saved.

Because God knows I'm going to do everything in my power to keep her dad from canceling on her for Christmas, and even if he does, even if some annoying punk kid who's in love with his daughter can't stop him from hurting her, she's not going to be alone on Christmas morning. She's not going to be heartbroken and she's not going to go to the pond by herself and she's not going to fall through the ice.

Not now that I can stop it.

Epilogue

***

"**D**ad, hurry up and get dressed, she's going to be here soon."

"I am dressed."

"A Christmas robe that lights up is *not* dressed."

"What do you mean? It's festive."

"Mom!"

Mom breezes into the family room carrying a plate of hot-from-the-oven sticky buns. "Tom, don't embarrass Graham in front of his girlfriend."

"Piper's going to have to learn sooner or later what she's getting into if she wants to be a part of this family."

Mom laughs. "They've only been on a few dates and you're already talking like they're engaged."

"Yeah, but he looks at her the way I look at you," Dad says, grabbing her hand and pulling her in.

Mom playfully pushes him away. "Tom, stop!"

"Trust me," Dad says, locking his hands at the small of her back and meeting her gaze. "A boy looks at a girl like that, he's in it for the long haul."

I shake my head but only because I know it'll freak out Mom if I tell her Dad's right. I don't know what my future holds—where I'll go to college or what I'll do with my life—but I know I want Piper to be there for all of it, and I want to be there for everything she does too.

Every single moment of it, to be exact.

The doorbell rings.

"I'll get it," I say, ducking out of the room before my parents start doing something embarrassing, like making out.

I check my reflection in the entryway mirror. Dad catches me and gives a knowing glance. I turn away from him, take a deep breath, and open the door.

"Hi," Piper says.

Her hair falls in waves past her shoulders, and her nose and cheeks are pink from the cold. She has a bundle of presents in her arms, wrapped in brown paper and tied with kitchen twine. Snowflakes drift lazily around her, catching on the white cable-knit sweater peeking out from underneath her coat.

"Hey, you," I say, pulling her in for a kiss.

Her lips curve into a smile as they press against mine. I love the warmth of her breath in my mouth, the gentle curling of her fingers around my neck. I could kiss her forever and not get enough.

In the days that followed my return, I could feel my brain trying to convince me that it had to have been a dream— that wishes made on shooting stars don't come true. That the entire world wouldn't get turned upside down just for one kid in Christmas, Virginia to change his life and save another. Believing it was a dream certainly would have been a more comforting thought than knowing that in another reality, in a place where different choices had been made, Piper—loving, daring, fierce-hearted Piper—had been ripped from this earth.

But while I was no longer with Sarah in this reality, all of the big things stayed the same, and I knew for sure that it hadn't been a dream.

Piper wore that same outfit—the skirt with the boots and the sweater—for her first day of work at the bookstore and Jordan still hit on her, but I'd already asked her to go to a movie with me that night, so she declined.

We still drew up plans for our parade float over hot chocolate at Nora's Ice Cream Parlor, and we still walked underneath her umbrella to the bowling alley, rain spitting sideways. I still taught her how to bowl, only this time I paid for all of the food and I jumped up and down with her when she scored her first strike. Sarah still texted me that night, but just to ask a homework question. When I told her I was on a date, she sent me a gif of a girl freaking out, followed by: TEXT ME EVERYTHING WHEN YOU GET HOME. I MEAN IT. ALL. THE. DETAILS.

We still talked about Piper's parents as we walked through snow-covered pines. When we happened upon Old Man Turlington's pond, I promised I'd take her skating in January, when the ice was thick enough to be safe.

We still danced in the barn to Patrick Swayze's "She's Like the Wind", only this time, instead of pulling away, I kissed her and asked her to be my girlfriend.

I didn't go to the dance with Sarah. I went with Piper. She still wore the same heart-stoppingly beautiful dress, and we still shared a carriage ride with Sarah and Jeremy, but the night was everything it should have been the first time around, and even though I knew it might have been too early to say such things aloud, I couldn't hold it in any longer. I told Piper I was falling in love with her while the snow fell down around us in front of her grandma's house. She said she was falling for me too, and I swear no moment has ever felt more perfect.

Sarah was still Christmas queen, but Jeremy wasn't king. He wasn't even in the court. He sat next to me on the steps in front of city hall and watched Sarah dance the part of Clara in the parade, then cheered her on when she reappeared in the second-to-last float wearing her crown. I whooped and hollered for Piper, who danced with the other cheerleaders, then we all went for hot cocoa at Nora's after.

While we were there, Piper got the call from her dad that he wouldn't be making it for Christmas this year. I put my arm around her and pulled her close, resting my lips against her forehead.

"You can come over to my house in the morning," I told her. "Queenie too."

"Your parents don't want some girl they barely know there."

I pulled back. "Seriously? My mom's been waiting for me to get a girlfriend since the day I was born."

"She has not."

"Has too. She's got all of this pent-up smothering saved specifically for this very occasion."

She bit her lip, thinking.

"Really," I said. "I insist you be there bright and early."

She arched a brow. "How early?"

"We start at seven."

She rolled her eyes. "Now I know for a fact that no one wants a stranger showing up at their house at seven o'clock in the morning."

"Have you met my mother? She's usually got half the house cleaned and two dozen cookies in the oven by seven."

"It's true," Jeremy said, stealing the candy cane from Sarah's cocoa and sticking it in his mouth.

Sarah pinched his cheek and stole it back.

I could tell Piper was waffling, so I said, "If you aren't there by seven, I'm going to show up at your house and put you in the car myself."

"All right," she'd said, leaning her head on my shoulder and grinning, and I don't know if all thoughts of her dad, of the divorce, of how Christmas should have been if her parents were still together, were gone, but at least I knew she'd be with me come Christmas morning, and nowhere near that pond.

"Where's Queenie?" I ask her now as she hands me the presents and steps inside.

"She's coming over later. Apparently your mom had already invited us for Christmas dinner."

"Awesome. Does Queenie mind if I just keep you for the day, then?"

Piper takes my hand and leans into my arm. "I'm all yours."

I press my lips against her temple and revel in the warmth of her skin, the hush of her breath. I think about a church on Christmas Eve, about wishes answered and unanswered. About life and destiny and second chances, and about a plan underpinning it all, something hinted at, woven, strung together from one moment to the next, from every chance meeting to every random happenstance.

If I've learned anything from my miracle, it's that there's no such thing as a perfect life. There's the life you currently have, the life you *think* you should have, and the life you *could* have, if you didn't spend your time wishing for something else. But there are perfect moments, the sort of moments you want to capture—on camera, in your mind, in eternity—and this, with Piper's head on my shoulder, her body leaning against mine, her jasmine perfume wrapping around me, is one of them.

All I want for Christmas, I think as we walk into the family room, hand in hand, Christmas lights twinkling and my parents opening their arms to welcome Piper into our home, *is right here.*

And it's perfect.

A Look At:
All I Want For Christmas is
the girl in charge

It's the holiday season in this young-adult contemporary romance, and all Beckett Hawthorne wants is to make his way across the country and try to find some semblance of a life that looks nothing like his past...until he meets Evelyn Waverly.

Evelyn Waverley, Christmas High's Senior Class President, volunteer at every Christmas charity drive, and basic overachiever, has a problem – she's co-directing and starring in her dream role as Elizabeth Bennet in her high school's production of A Pride and Prejudice Christmas, but Greg Bailey, the boy who was supposed to play Darcy broke his leg.

Enter Beckett Hawthorne, Aunt Bee's nephew, former child prodigy, and recent juvenile delinquent. Beckett has arrived in Christmas, Virginia to spend his community service hours working at his uncle's Christmas tree farm, as well as to get away from his heroin-addicted mother and abusive stepfather.

Of course, Beckett doesn't have any interest in the role of Darcy either, but when he (mistakenly) mentions the play to his social worker, she presses him to do it. He agrees to play Darcy, not expecting Evelyn's joyful attitude about life and all things Christmas to melt the permafrost that has formed around his heart. Soon he finds himself imagining a very different kind of future, one that is filled with the sorts of things he always thought were too good for him—hope, love, family—and he has Evelyn to thank for it.

AVAILABLE NOVEMBER 2021

Acknowledgements

✳ ✳ ✳

As always, I must thank God first. He gave me the idea for this story and faithfully saw me through its crafting in the nooks and crannies of my days over the course of several years. Then, in a pandemic year full of so much uncertainty, He brought me the opportunity to work with the amazing team at Wise Wolf, ensuring that I would not only see my dream come true of getting this book published, but that I would also see three other books of my heart published alongside it. I am so honored and humbled to have been granted the blessing of spending my writing days with the delightful cast of characters in this Christmas series, and to have reveled in the beauty, hope, light, and goodness of Christmas through them. What a blessing this journey has been.

Next, I must thank the two biggest earthly champions in this book's corner: my agent, Andrea Somberg, who has always seen me through every hill and every valley in my career, and who has now ushered three of my books into the world, with three more to come; and my editor, Rachel Del Grosso, who gave me the greatest gift the day she offered to publish this series. Working with you has been an absolute dream, just as working with everyone else at Wise Wolf—Lauren, Kristin, Mandi, Sam, and Laura—has been. I could not ask for a better, more supportive, more enthusiastic, or more brilliant team. Thank you all for everything that you do, and for all that you are. Authors and readers need more people like you pursuing, polishing, and publishing the books that will shape this generation and the generations to come.

To my writing friends who are always there to lend a sympathetic ear and a bastion of support—Nova McBee, Lori Goldstein, Natalie Mae, Lorie Langdon, Naomi Hughes, Marlena Graves, Ellen McGinty, Elizabeth Van Tassel, and all of the authors over at KidLitNet Café—God blessed me immeasurably when He brought you all into my life.

To Jane, for stepping in and helping with the kids so that I could carve consistent writing time into my days. This series would not be happening if it weren't for you (nor would my career, for that matter, if you hadn't been the one to guide me into it in the first place). Know that my heart will always be bursting with gratitude for you all the days of my life.

To Mom—I can't begin to count the number of ways you have supported me throughout my life, but know that I hold each and every instance in my heart, and that I would not be the woman I am without you. Your love has carved the stepping stones of my life, leading me to the places I always wanted to go, all because you told me I could get there. And to Dad, for saying you needed to get a bigger bookcase to display my books once you heard about this series, and for always being my biggest fan. Your constant support and encouragement fill me with a heaven-sent joy I cannot contain.

To Nathan, for your unending love and support. You are every romantic hero I write; the answer to my every childhood prayer; the other half of me; the soul to which my soul is tied. It never goes unnoticed that you are perpetually looking for ways to lift me up so I can shine. You are the perfect example of what true love looks like.

And to Emerson and Caleb, my sweet babies, my very heart split in two, I thank God every day for you, my precious ones, and I pray that you will always be attuned to the miracles that surround you in the patterns and rhythms of your days. God's love for you is written into every blade of grass, into every tree, into every breath you take, into every shooting star. Never forget that He is always with you, and that He is always for you.

And finally, to my readers. As long as a book is being written, it belongs to the author and to the One Who sustains its creation, but once it is published, it becomes yours. It is my deepest prayer that this book, and this series, would be one of the many tools God uses to bring you comfort, joy, and peace this holiday season.

God bless you all.

About the Author

***

Chelsea Bobulski is a graduate of The Ohio State University with a degree in history, although she spent more of her class time writing stories than she should probably admit. Autumn is her favorite time of the year, thanks to college football, falling leaves, cozy fireplaces, and the countdown to the most magical holiday of them all: Christmas. She is the author of *The Wood* (2017) and *Remember Me* (2019). She grew up in Columbus, Ohio, but now resides in northwest Ohio with her husband, two children, and one very emotive German Shepherd/Lab mix.

CPSIA information can be obtained
at www.ICGtesting.com
Printed in the USA
LVHW091959211022
731248LV00004B/340

9 781953 944115